TRADE SECRET OF A
OF A
MESSY RELATIONSHIP

UNDER SEATTLE'S SKY SERIES

OTHER BOOKS BY FRANCES BLACKTHORN

Under Seattle's Sky

Trade Secret of a Messy Relationship
This Little Thing Called Love
Thinking Out Loud

Broken Path

Tainted

TRADE SECRET
OF A
MESSY RELATIONSHIP

UNDER SEATTLE'S SKY SERIES

FRANCES BLACKTHORN

PROLOGUE

PETRA

Picture this: I'm in the house where I grew up, the one place that's always been my rock, and there's my brother, basically giving me the boot. Talk about a plot twist, right? Our parents left us way too soon in a car crash, and since then, it's just been Caleb and me, riding the rollercoaster of life. Well, that's what I thought, anyway.

Once upon a time, Caleb and I were inseparable – think Batman and Robin levels of tight. But life's been a real beast since Mom and Dad died, and suddenly, we're like strangers. Enter stage left: Joyce. *Oh, Joyce.* She's bad news with a capital B, and she's got about as much love for me as I have for a toothache.

Then Caleb drops this bombshell – he wants his new queen bee, Joyce, to move in. And guess who's gotta scram? *Yours truly.*

"Petra, you've got Deborah," he says like he's handing me a lottery ticket. "I gotta live my life too."

Please, cue the violins.

"Live your life? Caleb, what about our life? The one we've had since we were kids?" I throw back at him, feeling my blood boil.

"It's not the same, Petra. Joyce... she's different. I want this. I need this," he says, avoiding my gaze.

"Different? She's a hurricane in heels, Caleb! Since when do you bail on family for a fling?"

"A fling? She's more than that." He fires back, "And let's not forget, you're the one who ditched me first for your picture-perfect life. You've got it all – the perfect friends, the dreamy boyfriend, the job that's like the cherry on top."

I'm staring at him, feeling like I've just been slapped with a wet fish. "Bailing on you? Really? Last I checked, I wasn't the one turning our family home into some lovers' retreat for a girl who'd rather spit on me than say hello!" I take a breath, trying to steady my racing heart, and drop the bombshell, "And for the record, I don't have a fucking boyfriend anymore, so there goes your perfect picture."

Caleb's face flickers with surprise, like he's just been thrown a curveball he didn't see coming. "No boyfriend? What happened to Mr. Dreamy?"

Did he just call Douglas Mr. Dreamy?

"That's none of your business!" I snap back.

"You're overreacting, Petra." Caleb tries to reason, but his words feel hollow.

"Overreacting? No, Caleb. This is me waking up. You've changed, Caleb. You're not the guy I grew up with, the one who'd have my back no matter what."

His face hardens. "Maybe I have changed. Maybe it's about time I did."

That's when I know. This isn't just about Joyce or me. It's about us, about everything we've lost and can't find anymore.

"I don't even know who you are these days, Caleb. And frankly? I'm done trying to figure it out," I say, my voice cold.

I grab my stuff, cutting through the tension like a knife. No teary exit, no dramatic goodbyes. Just the sound of the door slamming shut behind me.

It hurts, like hell. But sometimes, you've gotta let go, even if it's the only family you have left.

CHAPTER ONE

PETRA

He's like something out of a dream, or maybe a really good, bad dream. The kind where you wake up and you're not sure whether you want to go back to sleep or stay awake. The moment he walks in, it's like the whole room takes a collective breath. It's as if the universe decided, 'Hey, let's make everyone else look dull,' and then there he is. He's got that movie star look, overflowing bank account, and the kind of charm that's almost illegal.

He's like a modern-day Adonis, all sun-kissed skin, dark, tousled hair, and a beard that's just the right side of rugged. It screams 'touch me,' and trust me, it takes everything in me not to reach out. And those eyes, damn, they're like a pair of emerald fires, blazing with an intensity that could scorch your soul. They pull you in, and suddenly, you're like, 'Breathing? What's that?'

I'm standing here, practically holding my breath, wishing I could just inhale normally again. But no, he has to go and make simple things like breathing feel like an Olympic sport.

Who am I talking about? You ask. *Rodrigo fucking Gomez.* Out of every jerk in the jerk store, why did it have to be him?

He's like that itch right in the middle of your back, the one you can't quite reach no matter how hard you try.

He's the kind of dream that lingers in the back of your mind long after you've woken up, the kind you can't shake off no matter how many cups of coffee you down. And here he is, swaggering into the room like he owns the place, stirring up memories I thought I'd locked away for good. It's like fate's up there, laughing its head off, bringing back old ghosts just when I thought I'd finally laid them to rest.

Standing here, seeing him again, it's a real test of willpower, I'll give you that. It's a toss-up between losing my cool and lunging at him — and not in the angry-cat kind of way, more like the 'pounce because I can't help it' kind. Every second he's here, it's a battle, one minute I'm thinking about how much I want to throttle him, and the next, how much I want to... well, let's just say the thoughts are less than pure.

We've been doing this dangerous tango on the tightrope between love and hate, crossing that line like a couple of daredevils, leaving nothing behind but the echo of our fireworks. And now, I'm expected to just play it cool, like we're a pair of strangers with nothing more than a shared past. But let's be real — Rodrigo Gomez and I are anything but strangers. Pretending otherwise is like trying to ignore the elephant in the room. No amount of make-believe can erase the fact that Rodrigo left his mark on me, a scar that's as much a part of who I am as the very air I breathe.

I shoot him a look sharp enough to cut, but he's in his own world, giving me one of those glances that's more of a brush-off, his attention flipping back to Pedro like I'm part of the wallpaper.

Pedro's the soon-to-be-married charmer, and then there's Rodrigo — his brother, but like the universe decided to sprinkle extra trouble on him. As I'm trying to figure out how two siblings can be so different, in swoops Deborah, my lifeboat in a sea of chaos, and Pedro's better half. She pops up, her arms wrapping around me in a bear hug that could probably bring the dead back to life.

"Gotcha!" Deborah beams, yanking my bag away like she's saving me from a tidal wave.

"Whoops, shit, Petty. Here, I got this," Pedro chimes in, swooping in with the grace of a knight, taking the load off my arms. He walks over to the couch with that gentle care that's all Pedro, placing the box down like it's made of glass. And there it is, the contrast between the Gomez brothers: Pedro, the golden boy with a heart of gold, and Rodrigo, the one who probably pawned his heart for a good joke and a smirk.

Rodrigo's doing his best statue impression, all propped up against the kitchen counter with his hands shoved in his pockets like he's guarding his family jewels. He's got that 'I'm up to no good' look on his face, stroking his beard like he's plotting world domination – or at least how to make my life more complicated. Meanwhile, Deborah and Pedro are in full helpful mode, chatting and chuckling as they unpack the boxes.

"Did I actually need all this stuff?" I muse out loud, snagging my old leather backpack from the pile. "You guys can chill, seriously. I've got two hands and a pulse. I can handle it."

But Deborah's not having any of my independence talk. She's already stacking boxes like Tetris blocks. "Oh, honey, let me be the martyr here," she says with that glint in her eye.

I shoulder my backpack, a bag of clothes in each hand, and make my way down the hall. I glide past Rodrigo, who's still as immobile as ever, his eyes drilling into me with that 'I'm so amused by your life choices' vibe. He's the kind of guy who could set your heart on fire, but I've played with fire before and I'm not looking to get burned again.

I'm hauling my life down the hallway to the room Deborah and Pedro set up for me when I catch this muttered "What the fuck?" floating behind me. It's got Rodrigo's trademark blend of disdain all over it.

Deborah's voice slices through my Rodrigo-induced fog. "You joining me or you gonna grow roots there?" she calls out.

"Yeah, I'm coming," I call back, staggering into the room under the weight of my worldly possessions. I plop down, trying to play it cool but I'm about as subtle as a bull in a China shop. "Rodrigo's back, huh?" I try to sound indifferent, but my voice betrays me, quivering like a violin string.

Deborah's got no clue about the can of worms that's my history with Rodrigo. I'm praying she doesn't pick up on the undercurrents of my questions while she's busy emptying boxes. "Yep, he's back. New office's up and he's Mr. Big Shot CEO," she says, tossing it out there like it's no big deal. *BUT IT IS.*

"Oh, is that so? Good for him," I manage to say, trying to sound as if I'm talking about the weather and not the storm that's just walked back into my life. Inside, I'm churning. "He's just here for the grand opening, right? Not like he's putting down roots or anything..." I add, a little too eagerly, picturing a countdown until he disappears again.

Deborah pauses, giving me a look that could mean she's onto me. "Why, you interested?" she probes, her eyebrow arching so high it's practically waving at me.

I flash her my best 'who, me?' smile. "Interested? Psh, no. Just making conversation," I say, trying to sound nonchalant. But who am I kidding? My interest in Rodrigo's comings and goings is about as casual as a heart attack.

Deborah eyes me like I'm a puzzle she's determined to solve. "Petty, spill it. Was there anything...ever...between you and Rodrigo?" She's got her arms folded, and eyebrow cocked – full-on detective mode.

"Oh, come on, Dee. Nothing to spill. He's been off the grid for ages, and our paths crossed, what, twice? He jetted off to Spain, did a New York minute, and poof— gone." I try to keep it breezy, rummaging for a box cutter, but my heart's doing the tango.

Except I'm fibbing. We were a thing. A big, messy, crash-and-burn kind of thing. I feel Deborah's gaze, sharp and probing, but I'm a vault, all business with the box in my hands. No way am I trotting out those skeletons.

She's still not convinced but lets it slide. "What are you hunting for?"

"A weapon of choice," I quip, with a smirk. "Something sharp and effective, like, I don't know, a machete? Or, better yet, a flamethrower." A flamethrower would be perfect – for torching old subjects, obliterating past mistakes, and... well, if Rodrigo got a little singed in the process, whoops. My bad.

—

I squint at the mountain of bags and boxes cluttering up my brother's place. "What the fuck? Is Petra setting up camp for an apocalypse or what?" It's like walking onto the set of 'Hoarders' — bags, boxes, backpacks, and I swear there's everything but a sink.

"She's moving in," Pedro tosses the words over his shoulder as if he's commenting on the weather.

No kidding, Sherlock. I've already spotted the suitcase camping in the hallway and I'm pretty sure there's a soon-to-be toothbrush in the bathroom that screams 'I'm staying.'

"And you didn't think to give me a heads-up?" I keep my cool, hands buried in my pockets, face schooled into neutrality.

Pedro smirks, "Didn't think it mattered to you. It's been what, six years? You're over her, right?" His eyebrow arches, poking at wounds he knows haven't healed.

I'm not over her. Not even close. Avoiding Petra's been my full-time job since we split. And now she's here, an everyday ghost, a walking, talking reminder of everything I let slip through my fingers.

"It's not about mattering or not," I shoot back, my voice tight as I push off the counter and head for the fridge. "It's about having the option to avoid this soap opera." I fish out a beer, snatch the opener, and flick the cap off. "Now, thanks to you, I'll be taking a rain check on family dinners. Cheers for the heads-up, bro." I take a long swig, letting the cold bitterness wash over me.

Having Petra under the same roof as my brother and his soon-to-be wife isn't just inconvenient. *It's torture.*

"Suit yourself, Rod," Pedro shrugs. "But you can't dodge Petra forever, can you?"

"Who's dodging?" I scoff, tossing back the lie with ease. I am no dodging – I'm sprinting from her, from the mess inside me, and from our past.

"You're so full of shit," Pedro laughs softly, "You can't fool me. Man, I know you. You're just scared to face the truth that you're still–"

"Zip it, Pedro," I snap, cutting him off mid-sentence. "You don't know shit."

He leans in whispering. "Prove me wrong then, brother."

"Nothing to prove." I avert my gaze, pretending to be absorbed in anything but this conversation. "I'm just fine without her."

Pedro leans back, mock contemplation on his face. "Ever wonder where you got that charming personality?"

"Charming? That's just scratching the surface."

He laughs, but there's a bite to it. "I was also aiming more for 'spiteful and despicable, not exactly for Mr. Congeniality'."

I wave him off, "Hey, credit where it's due, big bro. You were the original jerk. I'm just the sequel." A smirk plays on my lips. "All those times you played the bully, you were crafting a masterpiece."

The corner of his mouth twitches, "Revisionist history, much? I was the mentor, you were the menace – a little terror."

I flash him a grin, "Wow, hold the applause. Your adoration's making me all warm and fuzzy." I steer away from the brotherly roast, heading towards the couch with purpose. "But let's get down to brass tacks. We gotta talk about business." I plop down on the couch, patting the seat next to me, signaling it's time to switch gears from barbs to business.

I lean back, all casual-like, watching Pedro claim the chair opposite me. "So, your empire, I'm assuming?" he quips, easing into the seat. He's got me pegged — my company is my world. It's my chaotic, beloved kingdom.

I tip back my beer, "The building is finally done, as you know, and people are getting comfy," I say, taking another swig. "Also, some of the staff who worked with me before agreed to come here, even if it's just for a while, which means I won't have to hire a lot of new people for now. But what I need—" I pause, eyes locking on his "—is a right-hand man. Someone who's got the chops for it. Someone like you."

"Rodrigo... no. You don't mean you want me to work for you, right?" Pedro leans in, eyebrows up.

I snort. "Hell no, man." I can practically hear his heart unclench. "You'd work WITH me. Side by side." I punch the air for emphasis, wanting him to grasp the gravity of it. "I'm not looking for a minion, Pedro. I want a co-conspirator, a brother-in-arms."

He's on his feet now. "No, Rodrigo. Just no."

I mimic his tone, "And WHY, pray tell, why not?"

I watch him as he towers over me. I'm ready to parry whatever reason he throws my way because this isn't just business. It's personal now.

Pedro's pacing like a caged animal, hands raking through his hair. "You know the score, Rodrigo. This isn't checkers — it's chess. And you're asking me to knock over my own king."

That was actually a perfect analogy.

I play dumb, leaning back with a smirk. "I'm just tossing you an invite to the cool kids' table. What's the drama?"

I'm fully aware of the family saga I'm poking at—our family's saga. I'm not just nudging him – *I'm flipping the board*. I know exactly what he's talking about. He's talking about the family business I'm not part of anymore. He's talking about loyalty, duty, and tradition.

"Rodrigo, I'm knee-deep in Dad's world. I work for him," he halts, a conflict playing out across his face. "I can't just—"

I cut him off with a laugh. "There's the rub. You work FOR him. With me, it's a partnership."

He's exasperated now, "You're missing the whole damn point."

"I'm just asking my brother, my flesh and blood, to work with me," I put the empty bottle on the white table in front of the couch. "Like the good old days, back-to-back, just you and me against the world," I pitch, standing to make my case, hands buried deep in my pockets. I throw my blazer over my shoulder, all casual-like. "No pressure. Mull it over." The offer hangs between us.

Pedro's voice trails after me. "It's not about wanting to or not. It's...you're the competition."

I spin on my heel, quick with the comeback. "It's about time you stopped being a pawn in his game and started playing your own."

He sighs, "I'll think about it."

"Take your time," I say, already halfway out the door. "Later, Dee!" I call without looking back.

Her distant "Bye!" is a sweet note in the chaotic symphony of family and business.

CHAPTER TWO

PETRA

My eyelids are staging a protest, refusing to open as my alarm clock unleashes its hellish wail. I've already slapped the snooze button twice – third time's the charm, right? *Dream on.* The universe, with its twisted sense of humor, demands I get up.

Dragging my body from the sheets, I stretch, cracking bones sounding off like a round of applause for the feat. The plush black rug greets my feet, a small mercy in the cruel ritual of dawn.

I fumble into the closet, cursing the darkness like it's a personal affront. My hands swipe the air, seeking the soft fabric of my go-to slippers, but alas, they remain elusive. With a sigh, I give up and head to the light switch near the door. I rifle through the hangers, my fingers finally landing on the holy grail of outfits – beige pants, black blouse, and stilettos. Mirror check – blouse tucked, pants straight, dignity intact. "You'll do," I mutter, ready to conquer. Or at least, not get conquered by the day ahead.

As I dive into the abyss that is my backpack, I can't help but scold myself. "Petra, darling, ever heard of unpacking?" But no, I had to play it cool, live out of a bag like I'm perpetually on the run. *Genius move.*

I waltz into the bathroom, my very own oasis of calm, and snatch up my makeup bag. I'm on a treasure hunt for the eyeliner and mascara that'll make my eyes pop. Foundation? Ha! As if I'd ever find the ghostly shade of my skin on any shelf.

Teeth – check. Fresh breath – double-check. I swoop up my trench coat and bag from the chair like I'm Cinderella at the stroke of midnight. Keys? Buried in the depths of my bag, because let's face it, they're the chariot to my very un-fairy-tale life.

Phone in hand – because who needs a screen that isn't spiderwebbed with cracks? – I strut out the door.

—

I pull into the lot, my Audi A1 Sportback gleaming like a panther in the morning sun. The office beckons, and as I stride in, there's Pedro, Mr. Sunshine himself, armed with an Everest of paperwork.

"Morning, Petty! You look... shockingly awake," he quips, that grin plastered on his face. He's well aware that 'morning person' is not in my vocabulary.

To say mornings and I mix like oil and water is putting it mildly. But Pedro? He gets it. He gets the love-hate tango I have with the break of day because, despite the torture of dawn, I'm a beast when it comes to my job.

And Pedro, he's the king of this castle, steering the family empire with that easy charm, but don't let that fool you. He's sharp, knows everyone and their secrets. As for me, I'm the silent storm, the ninja in the shadows. I'm the whisper of a threat in every deal – when I move, it's already done. Pedro might steer this ship, but we all know who's carving the path through the waves.

"How is my favorite paralegal today?" he teases, looking over his shoulder and giving me a warm smile.

"Alive... barely. Dreaming of a caffeine." I toss back, the words thick with my need for that dark, bitter elixir of life. "And how's my favorite boss?"

He spins, all suave CEO, and fires back, "The boss is about to sprint for a meeting with the clock, and as thrilling as your AM snark is, duty calls." He's always in a hurry, always busy, always on the go.

I head towards my desk, the one tucked in the corner with a view of the action, placing my bag on my desk and turning on the computer before heading upstairs for my much-needed caffeine fix. Coffee's my sidekick, my knight in shining armor, the Clark Kent to my Lois Lane. It's not just a beverage – *it's a lifeline.*

There are some rooms that aren't open-concept in this place – this is a combination of open space and private rooms like both bosses' offices, the conference hall, and the holy grail of break rooms, which suits me just fine.

As I trudge up the white granite stairs, I glide by Pedro's office. He's in deep with some mystery guest while Avery, our admin ninja, does the office equivalent of a drive-by, tapping on the door before vanishing inside. I stick my head into the conference room, playing peek-a-boo with the empty chairs. Pedro's hinted apocalypse must be running on a delay.

In the kitchen, I get a mug, christening it with the sacred bean juice from the machine. The scent's a punch of wake-the-hell-up, and I'm here for it. One sip of the black gold, and it's hello world. Another, and I'm ready to dance.

Strutting out, coffee in hand, I catch a glimpse of the big boss, Mr. Gomez himself, strolling out of Pedro's office. Getting closer, I hear him mutter under his breath, "Of course he is late. Una vez niño, siempre niño," shooting me a look that could either be 'Good morning' or 'Watch yourself, kiddo.' Before I can decode it, he's ducking back into the office, with Pedro giving me the old stink-eye before slamming the door.

Who's he calling a child? My Spanish is rusty, but I'm betting 'niño' doesn't mean 'responsible adult.'

Stumbling down the stairway like it's my first time on two legs, I collide with an immovable object, or more precisely, an immovable someone. "Oh, shit!" I exclaim as I watch the coffee tsunami on the pristine white steps. "I am so sorry!" I babble, only to look up and see the coffee apocalypse has hit Rodrigo square in his shirt.

Yep, the universe has a sick sense of humor. Of course, it's Rodrigo, coffee-drenched and looking like a storm cloud in human form. Because why not? If my morning was going to implode, might as well be a spectacle.

"Bite me," I mutter, barely a whisper, hoping he didn't catch it.

But of course, he does. "As tempting as that sounds, Bird, I'll pass." *His sneer is so punchable.* "Is it like a paid gig for you? Spilling coffee on unsuspecting visitors?"

"Trust me, your highness, your ego isn't worth the coffee I'd lose."

He pauses his ascent up the stairs to shoot me that look, "Just so you know, this shirt is worth more than your little coffee mishap."

"I'm sure you'll survive. There's a whole world of overpriced shirts out there. Or, I don't know, try going shirtless. Might do the world some good."

Great, Petra, now you've done it.

He quirks a brow, an unreadable glint in his eyes. "Careful, Bird, keep talking like that, and I might do it for you. You just have to ask nicely."

"In another life, maybe," I retort, trying to keep my cool as he gives me that top-to-toe appraisal that makes my skin prickle—in a not entirely unpleasant way.

He flashes a grin, "Try to have a day as delightful as you are, Bird." The wink he sends me is like a bolt, setting my face aflame.

"Maybe you should change your shirt. You don't want to stain your reputation." I'm really hoping I'm getting the last word here.

But Rodrigo just laughs, that infuriatingly charming laugh. "Nah, I'll keep the stain. It's a conversation starter — 'you should see the other guy', I'll say." He taps the dark spot on his shirt, a mock salute, and strides off.

I'm left standing there, half-mad, half... something else. *Damn him.*

—

RODRIGO

Of course, Petra's part of this corporate circus now. I didn't know that when I jetted off to Spain. She wasn't in the picture then, not until Pedro dropped her name casually into a convo in New York, two years after I'd left.

Pedro cracks his office door open, his voice slicing through the air, "Ever think of, I don't know, not being at odds with him for once?" His gaze drops to the coffee catastrophe on my chest. "And for the love of all that's holy, what's with the shirt? What happened?"

"Petra," I mutter, brushing by him into his office. "Petra happened to my shirt. A 'Petra incident', if you will," I add with a shrug.

"Rodrigo, llegas tarde," Dad chimes in, his frown deep as the Mariana Trench. "How do you expect to do business looking like you've just tumbled out of a cab?"

Pedro, ever the mediator, jumps in, "Why don't we take this to the conference room?"

But Dad's having none of it. "Look at that shirt. Did you lose your manners in New York?"

Ah, the joys of family business. "You know, your team has this knack for hospitality," I start, sarcasm dripping from every syllable. "Offered me a steaming cup of coffee, and who am I to say no? But then, the stairs and I had a disagreement, and the coffee chose the stairs' side." I catch Pedro's skeptical look. "Racing home to change would've only made me later. Can't have that on your watch, right, Papá?" I enter the conference room, leaving a trail of my father's mutters in my wake.

As I slump into the chair, my inked knuckles come to rest on the gleaming table, prompting a scowl from the big boss. Tattoos might as well be hieroglyphs to him – symbols of rebellion, signs I've strayed off his straight path. They're his pet peeves, reminders of the chasm between his starched collar world and mine. He sees them as my life's blemishes, indelible marks of defiance. *It's almost poetic, really.*

Pedro's got his CEO face on, all business at the helm of the table with his tech arsenal spread out. I toss him a look that says, 'Let's do this shit,' and pivot to the main act, my father.

"What's on the table, Rodrigo?" Dad's tone is practically bristling with suspicion, his eyes sharp on me.

Trust him to mix a cocktail of paternal doubt with professional critique. Yeah, he is my father, but at moments like these? He's the maestro of the 'you're not good enough' symphony, the guy who made my last name feel like a heavyweight title I never asked for.

I force a Zen breath through the tension, keeping my voice steady. "I've got a golden ticket for us, one that'll line your pockets and sweeten the deal on your end," I say, the edges of my mouth curling into a salesman's grin.

Dad leans back, arms folded, the picture of reluctant intrigue. "Estoy escuchando," he signals, giving me the floor.

I tossed the idea to Pedro, kinda like throwing a match into a dry forest, half-expecting it to ignite – it was simple, I wanted him to work with me. He shot back with a wild card – 'let's deal Dad into this game'. *I almost laughed.* Strike a deal with the old lion? But hell, I went along. Who knows, maybe Dad had mellowed out enough to actually listen, to see the vision. So, we decided to roll the dice and see if the big boss would come to the table.

Fast forward, and here I am, laying it out for Dad, "I need Pedro and part of your crew. My empire's growing, and I want the family crest on this new chapter."

Dad chuckles like I've told the joke of the century. "Oh, so you're poaching now? Planning a corporate heist under my nose?"

I stand, the chair screeching its protest. "Not poaching, collaborating. Think of it as a merger of talents. I've got the playground, and you've got the players. I want to expand the services my company offers, and you have something I don't have yet here in Seattle."

Dad's silent, his eyes tracking me as I make my case, rolling up my sleeves like I'm about to get my hands dirty. *Which, metaphorically, I am.*

I start, arms crossed, a half-grin playing on my lips. "Imagine this – a merger. Our companies, joining forces. It's like the dream team coming together."

My father's eyebrow quirks up, "And why would I do that? Hand over the keys to my kingdom to a kid."

I chuckle, "Because, querido Papá, while you've been playing king of the hill, I've been conquering the valley. My New York office? It's the David to your Goliath, and guess what? David's on a winning streak."

Pedro coughs, a poorly disguised snort of amusement, and I shoot him a quick, knowing look.

Dad leans forward, his eyes narrowing. "You're saying you're a threat to me?"

I nod, slow and deliberate. "Big time. But it doesn't have to be a showdown at high noon. Join forces, and we become untouchable. Stay separate, and well," I shrug, "May the best man win."

Silence stretches between us, the tension thick enough to cut with one of those fancy letter openers on his desk.

"What's in it for me?" Dad finally asks, his tone guarded yet curious, like a chess player contemplating his next move.

"Survival, prosperity, legacy," I say, ticking them off on my fingers. "And the chance to say you partnered with the king of the world."

Dad's lips twitch, almost a smile, and I know I've got him.

"My team's golden touch, your name in the spotlight – seriously, who wouldn't want a piece of that action?" I flash a cocky smile, just to rile him up a bit more.

Dad folds his arms, unimpressed, but I can tell I've piqued his interest. "You think too highly of yourself, mijo."

I laugh, shaking my head. "Not high – accurate. I've got a client list that's the envy of the industry. They're all lining up, checkbooks open, ready to throw money at us. We team up, and bam! We're the dream team. You get the fame, the clients, and the satisfaction of being part of something epic."

"And why exactly would I need you for that?" Dad's trying to play it cool, but the curiosity is there, lurking behind his poker face.

I stand tall, all business now. "Your IP department – it's the missing puzzle piece I need. And let's not forget Pedro here. Guy's a people magnet. He's got that HR magic, solving problems like a pro. We combine your muscle with my flair, and we're unstoppable."

"I don't do deals with the devil, son." Dad says.

"Well, good thing I'm just a businessman with a devilish charm then. And you, doing business with yourself? That'd be a real hellish ordeal, wouldn't it?"

Pedro jumps in. "Let's put a pin in it, huh? Give it some thought, sleep on it."

I grab my blazer from the back of the chair, slipping into it. "Cool. Take your time. Let's circle back in a week. We'll see if you're ready to play in the big leagues." With a nod and a smirk, I'm out the door, leaving them with a proposition too tempting to ignore.

CHAPTER THREE

PETRA

As the sound of footsteps echoes down the staircase, I casually glance up, and there's Rodrigo in all his morning disaster glory. He's sporting a shirt with a fresh coffee badge of honor, and his blazer's just a reluctant accessory draped over one arm. He's got that 'just dodged a boardroom blitz' look, and it's doing things to my pulse that should probably be illegal.

My heart decides it's time for a sprint, palms acting like they're in a sauna. Seriously, why does this guy have my body on high alert?

His eyes pin me down, and I'm as transparent as glass under his gaze. No mystery left — just me, my racing heart, and a blush I can't control. I make a valiant attempt to look anywhere but at him, searching desperately for a distraction, *any distraction*. But nope, the universe is not that kind. With a twist of my head, a feeble attempt at indifference, I can still feel the intensity of his stare, like he's a hunter and I'm the prize. Sneaking another look his way, I catch him still staring, an unblinking sentinel.

His ringtone breaks the spell and he whips out his phone, his brows knitting together as he walks away to take the call. "Shit," I mutter under my breath, the tension in my shoulders dropping away.

Suddenly, Bea's hushed tone buzzes in my ear. "Whoa, who's that hottie?" My heartbeat thunders on, a traitor to my feigned disinterest.

"Hot? Around here? You must be mistaken," I deflect, but my shaky voice is a dead giveaway.

Bea steps into view, a vision of poise and radiance, her brown skin glowing against her crisp white top, her braid a sleek cascade, her makeup impeccable. "Oh, come on. He was totally checking you out."

I can hear my own heart drumming as Bea's words ricochet in my head. Rodrigo had indeed made me his prime-time show. "Rodrigo? Oh, that's just Pedro's brother," I toss off, praying my voice doesn't betray the sudden surge of adrenaline.

"Is it like a requirement in the Gomez family to be off-the-charts hot? They're like walking, talking cologne ads, I swear." Her gush has me stifling a laugh.

I have to slam the brakes on her fan club meeting. "Bea, please, stop it. My stomach's doing backflips, and not in a good way."

She shoots me a glare that could curdle milk, but I flash her my best 'oops' smile. With a dramatic roll of her eyes, she's off to resume her 'tragically ordinary' existence.

As the clock ticks on, I'm buried in work until Pedro's voice booms from upstairs, yanking me back to reality. "Petra, a sec?" he's half-hovering on the staircase.

"Sure thing," I chirp, phone in pocket, poker face on.

I ascend to Pedro's office, where the big boss is. "We need your savvy for a company game-changer," Pedro says.

I nod, all ears. *What's this all about?*

———

I feel stressed out as I stroll out of the office. Dad and me, we mix like oil and water, especially when it's about business, and even though I know my offer is a win-win for both of our companies, I also know he's not a fan of change. I made him an offer, a solid one, but he treats risks like they're hot coals. And when it's me tossing the dice? Forget about it.

As I go down the stairs, I spot Petra at her desk. She's changed so much, and at the same time, she's stayed the same. She's grown into a gorgeous, confident woman, but she still has the same sparkling eyes and sweet smile that captivated me years ago.

As my world's spinning from the meeting, I catch her eye. She's quick to look away, leaving me tangled in a web of what-ifs and should-nots. I'm itching to bridge the gap, to say something, anything, but my brain's short-circuiting.

My phone starts ringing, saving me from a potential crash and burn – *and it's Sofia*. My sister only dials my number when she's got a problem that apparently only I can fix.

"Hey, Sofia. Is everything okay?"

Her voice is a hurricane. "OKAY? Not even close. Saskya destroyed my red dress – the one I had on standby for Pedro's birthday party."

I just laugh. That dog got some sass. "And since when is my dog's taste for couture my problem?"

The phone's like a lit fuse on the other end, and Sofia's doing her best impression of a steam whistle. "Because she's your freaking dog, that's why! She's your responsibility, and this whole mess is your responsibility as well," she's practically spitting fire. "I said I would watch her today, but I didn't say I would babysit her every move and that she could chew on my stuff."

"Alright, breathe," I say, trying to dodge the bullets. "I'll sort it. A new dress for Pedro's party – consider it done. And I'll keep Saskya on a no-dress diet, pinky swear."

She's on a roll, demanding a clone of the casualty. "Red. Same as before."

"Yeah, got it," I'm already half out of the conversation, my mind on the next move. "Gotta go, work's calling."

She's not done. The blame's flying like arrows, and I'm the target. "This mess is on you! You careless prick."

I chuckle, swinging into my car. "Oh please. The only thing careless was you leaving your wardrobe open as a doggy buffet. And Saskya's just got a keen eye for fashion disasters."

The line's sizzling now. "You're impossible!"

"Back at you, but hey, gotta run. Keep Saskya away from the wardrobe, yeah? And try some chew toys instead of couture." With that, I hit 'end call,' still grinning.

I hit the ignition and the engine purrs to life. I've got a pit stop to make at *Casa de Rodrigo*, courtesy of Petra's coffee-flinging antics – nothing like a wardrobe malfunction to spice up your morning.

I glide the car into the garage, leaving the blazer behind. No casualties there, thankfully. Up the stairs two at a time, and I'm peeling off the coffee-drenched shirt before it can offend any more sensibilities.

Into the bedroom, a quick detour to the bathroom to slam-dunk the shirt into the hamper. I flip through my closet with a mission. There, another white shirt, pristine and unsuspecting.

28

Here's to hoping it's not a coffee magnet.

—

PETRA

Mr. Gomez pins me with those piercing green eyes, the kind that could give you frostbite. "Ms. Smith, you're the manager of the formalities for the IP department, correct?" he probes, with a gravity that could sink ships.

I manage a "Yes, that's right," throwing a glance at Pedro for a lifeline.

He leans in, "You enjoy being part of this enterprise, Ms. Smith?" If his stare was intense before, it's laser now.

Panic knots my insides. Did I mess up somehow? Did my coffee habit bankrupt their supplies?

I'm spiraling, but Pedro's voice lassos me back to reality. "Petra?!"

Snapping back, I muster, "Oh, absolutely. This job is kind of my everything."

Mr. Gomez's gaze doesn't waver. "My boy here places a hefty bet on your instincts. So, enlighten us with your wisdom, will you?"

I just nod, mind racing. What the hell did I get myself into? *And Pedro, why'd you have to put your chips on me?*

"Ms. Smith, what would you do if you were running this business and someone offered a merger between two companies?" Mr. Gomez asks, not done yet. I wait for him to go on. "If someone with a big name in the industry, doing the same thing as you, came here and proposed a merger because they needed some of the people working for you to work for them too?"

"It's all about the fine print, Mr. Gomez. I'd need to weigh my gains against my losses, line by line."

"What if all they were giving you in return was their company name and list of clients, meaning you would share the same clients while they promised you that they wouldn't take business away from you?" Mr. Gomez asks — tricky, *tricky*.

"Even with a sweet promise like that, I'd need to tally up everything I'm putting on the line," I explain. "I'd have to make sure the scales balance out to a fair trade for both parties."

Mr. Gomez actually looks impressed. "Well, your thought process is top-notch, Ms. Smith."

I can't help myself — I have to know why we're playing hypotheticals. "Just out of curiosity, Mr. Gomez, how does my role here connect to this merger talk?" I ask, bracing for his answer.

"Because Ms. Smith, it seems that the other party really wants our Intellectual Property, both the formal and the technical teams, as part of this merger." Mr. Gomez drops the bombshell — it's not just theoretical chitchat. We're in merger territory for real.

"As big as our team is," I start, keeping my cool while my brain's running a marathon, "My gut's twisting over the thought of losing some of our best people to the other company."

"Hmmm," Mr. Gomez nods slowly and looks away for a moment before looking back at me. "But Ms. Smith, technically, after the merger, the other company will be part of our company, so they won't be the 'other company' anymore. Can we cross that off as a risk?"

"It's a leap of faith. Without knowing who we're dealing with on the other side, it's hard to say for sure what could or couldn't happen. Unless you can make new contracts for the team members that say they won't leave our company to work for the other party's branches, I don't see a way to safely go ahead with the merger."

Appreciation flickers in his eyes. "Your insights are valuable, Ms. Smith," he says, standing to shake my hand.

Heading for the door with a parting thanks from Pedro, I'm nearly home free when Mr. Gomez hits me with the million-dollar question – "Ms. Smith, one last thing. As the formalities head and as a paralegal in my company, how tempted would you be to leave your position and go work for another company?"

I take a beat, then play my hand. "Temptation's always there, Mr. Gomez. But like I said, it's all in the details." With a smile that doesn't reach my eyes, I slip out the door, leaving the what-ifs hanging in the air.

CHAPTER FOUR

RODRIGO

I'm finally done with work and ready to go home. Pedro's playing it cool, pretending our morning's meeting never happened, so I hit the ignition and dial him up, the Bluetooth doing its thing.

"Hey," he greets me casually. As if my patience isn't hanging by a thread.

I cut to the chase, "Spill it about the big boss's opinion on the merger, Pedro." He dodges, all 'hush-hush, can't talk shop now,' and I'm here revving my engine, literally and metaphorically. "Why the radio silence, bro?" I press.

"Ahm, I'm afraid I can't discuss the meeting at this time," he says evasively.

"Are you still at the office?"

"I'm just leaving now to head home," he says.

"Then, why the hell can't you talk about the meeting?" I ask, "Come on, stop beating around the bush," I urge him.

"Because it's business related, and there are a lot of things involved, like—"

"Business this, business that," I'm about to blow a gasket when, "Fine," I relent, cool as a cucumber on the surface while plotting my next move. "I'll swing by for dinner. Deborah's cooking, right?"

Pedro's caught off guard, "You're joking. You planning a dinner interrogation?"

Do I look like I'm joking? But I lay it on thick, "Just a friendly family meal."

"You and 'friendly family meals' don't mix. You don't do 'friendly'," he says.

"Hey, that's not true. Don't hurt my feelings," I joke.

"Fine, Rodrigo," he sighs. "I'll let Deborah know that you'll be stopping by."

Mission accomplished. I'll get my answers one way or another.

"Oh, and Saskya's my plus-one," I tell Pedro, grinning to myself. "Better than showing up solo, right?"

He's got that sarcastic edge in his voice, "Oh, joy. A drooling furball to spice up dinner."

We exchange goodbyes, and I'm off to scoop up my four-legged demolition expert. If anything can break the ice tonight, it's her wagging tail and canine charm.

—

I roll up to Pedro and Deborah's like I own the place, having just escaped a drama fest courtesy of my sister. You'd think Saskya had chewed up the Crown Jewels from the way Sofia carried on. As I bail out of my car, Saskya's hot on my heels, looking like butter wouldn't melt. She's got a thing for the family – acts like a total goof with Sofia, tolerates Dee in short sneezy bursts, and thinks Pedro's the sun, moon, and stars.

Buzzing myself into the building, we hit the stairs because let's be real, Saskya treats elevators like they're death traps. Three flights up, and I've torched more calories than a gym session.

Dee greets us, spoon in hand, ready to duel. "Make one wrong move…"

"I'm shaking," I retort, but I'm grinning because we all know she's got the reflexes of a napping cat.

Inside, Pedro's already fussing over Saskya, giving her the royal treatment. She's eating it up, tail going a mile a minute.

Pedro gets up and looks at me, "So, what's up?"

Deborah pipes up, "I have no clue 'what's up', but you've already hijacked our evening, might as well make yourself useful and help us set the table." She's smiling, but believe me, I know it's not a request.

"Careful, Dee. I've got a four-legged weapon here," I warn. "One whistle and you'll have more doggy drool than you can handle."

But there she goes, stacking plates and silverware in my arms like I'm the hired help. I take them, because the truth is, when it comes to family, you play the game or you get the spoon.

I'm counting plates, "Four? For who – oh." Lightbulb moment. Petra's living here now. *Crap.* Almost slipped my mind.

Deborah's giving me that 'Captain Obvious' look as she juggles pots and pans. "Because math, Rodrigo. We're four. You know, one, two, three, four?"

I throw her a mock salute. "And the fourth musketeer? Our dear Petra – where's she hiding?"

Deborah shrugs, the universal sign for 'don't ask me.' "Your guess is as good as mine. But I hope the table will be ready when the fourth musketeer walks in that door."

"Right, right," I nod, grinning, "Looks like we have a wild card in the mix."

—

I get home and stick my keys in the door. As I open it, I hear some chatter from inside, and I shut the door behind me and walk to the kitchen. "Ouch!" My butt's now best friends with the floor.

Deborah's "Shit, Petra!" blends with Pedro's concerned "Petty, are you okay?" But I'm too busy being slobbered on by a tongue that's found my face. *A dog?*

"Wow, I didn't expect to get a kiss from a stranger when I got home. What a nice surprise!"

"Sask!" I hear a rough voice say. "What are you doing?" I look up and spot Rodrigo looking at Sask like he's betrayed. "You little backstabber."

"Is this your dog?" I ask, wiping drool from my cheek.

"Nah, just met her. Named her Saskya on a whim. Love at first sight."

My eyes roll so hard I see my brain. Rejecting his outstretched hand, I hoist myself up. "You're hilarious. Did you swallow a comedian?"

"Nope, did you baptize anyone else in coffee today, or am I the chosen one?" he grins.

"Just you," I shoot back, the sarcasm dripping. I give Saskya a pat — traitorous beast — and march off for a pre-dinner de-dogging shower.

"Oh, so that's what you meant when you said 'she happened' to your shirt." Pedro nods in understanding.

"Yep, that's the shirt saga," I confirm with a sigh. "I'm going to shower now."

Saskya's tail is a wagging beacon of innocence, and I swear if looks could kill, Rodrigo would be six feet under for making me the butt of his joke. "Remember, ears are a magnet for stray hairs," he throws out.

Whipping around, I can't resist the jab. "I'll be sure to shed every last trace of you in the process."

His wink is infuriatingly smug. "You're just dying to keep a piece of me, aren't you, Bird?"

"In an alternate universe, maybe," I snap, the burn of my blush probably visible from space.

His declaration of crashing our dinner slams into me like a wrecking ball.

I stomp into my room, my bag and phone flying onto the chair like they've personally offended me. Heels clatter to the floor with the force of my mood. "Of all the gin joints, in all the towns, in all the world, he walks into mine," I mutter to the walls. Stripping down to my indignation, I scrub my face clear of the day's mask. "Six years of peace, and he swaggers back into town like the prodigal pain in my ass," I grumble to the accusing mirror. "Could've been a permanent vacation, but no, fate just loves a good joke."

I'm talking to my reflection like it's going to offer some groundbreaking advice. Rodrigo's probably out there, Mr. Casanova, not giving me a second thought, while I'm here having a meltdown to my bathroom tiles.

Hair yanked up in a bun that screams 'I've given up', I ditch the clothes and step into the shower. The water's embrace is the only thing that's right in my world right now. It's a liquid lullaby, and for a fleeting moment, I imagine it could just carry all my Rodrigo-induced aggravations right down the drain.

RODRIGO

"Cut to the chase, hermano. What's the verdict on Dad's corporate chess game?"

Pedro's rubbing his temples like I'm the human version of a migraine. "Rodrigo, really?" he grumbles, looking like he's one question away from bolting.

Dee, ever the instigator without meaning to be, leans in. "The big talk about the merger, right? Spill it."

I shoot Pedro a gotcha grin. "Look at that, even your better half's on the edge of her seat," I quip, all but batting my lashes from across their pristine kitchen setup.

Pedro's shooting daggers at Dee, who's all innocence and confusion. "What? I just asked," she protests.

"Sweet Dee, you're as faultless as they come," I assure her, pouring on the charm.

Pedro's exasperation is practically a tangible cloud in the room. "Fine, it was... okay," he finally speaks.

"I'm all apologies for breathing," Deborah deadpans.

"Don't sweat it, querida. Pedro's just got a flair for the theatrical," I chuckle, nudging the conversation back to the main event. "But come on, Pedro, dish out the dirt. What's the big bosses' stance on our empire's next chapter?"

"Alright," he caves. "Papá's not exactly jumping for joy at your grand scheme of company matrimony."

My jaw might as well be on the floor. "He's not biting? Seriously?" I slump onto a barstool like my strings have been cut. "I practically served our companies on a silver platter."

Pedro's leaning back like he's got all the answers. "You left some blanks in the master plan, genius."

I mirror him, incredulous. "Blanks? Like what, a secret escape hatch?"

He's casual as can be. "Like what will happen if you decide to poach the staff from Dad's company to your company."

I throw my hands up, exasperated. "Who would do that? And hey, remember? Contracts. It'll be one, big, corporate lovefest if he just says yes. I won't even need to offer new jobs to his team! His team will be my team."

Pedro's not budging. "Well, not exactly. You still have your precious New York company that you made sure Dad couldn't touch. Your untouchable New York baby."

I can't believe this. I lean back, staring at the ceiling, seeking divine patience. "Why didn't he throw that in my face during the showdown, then?"

"He didn't think of it then," Pedro shrugs.

"That's bullshit, and you know it," I growl, my temper flaring. "It's because I'm the one pitching, isn't it? He can't let go of the past, blind to the win-win."

Pedro hits me with a scoff. "You lecturing about letting go of the past? That's a good one. You and Dad collect grudges like they're limited-edition stamps."

The nerve. "Thanks a bunch. Now stop painting me with the same brush as him."

He throws his hands up in surrender. "Look, if you want my two cents – this merger's going nowhere fast. Dad's on snail mode."

I'm about ready to punch a wall, but I take a deep breath instead. Dee, the voice of reason, chimes in. "Someone go fetch Petra for dinner, will you?"

I snort. "Why bother? She can nuke her portion later."

"No, we wait for her," Deborah insists with that tone that brooks no argument.

Fantastic. I'm here starving, the deal's hanging by a thread, and we're on royal time. "Perfect. Just perfect."

Pedro grumbles and gets up to fetch Petra, but as if on cue, she waltzes in.

CHAPTER FIVE

PETRA

I storm into the kitchen, feeling the air crackle with tension. "Oh, look who's still here," I sneer as I see Rodrigo sitting at the island. "Don't you have a life?"

Rodrigo lifts his head and meets my gaze, walking towards me. He's tall enough to make me feel like a dwarf next to him. "I'm here for the same reason you are, sweetheart," he says, pointing to the roast beef on the stove. "It's dinner time, in case you've forgotten."

I cross my arms, a barrier against his looming presence. "I might forget names, dates, even faces — but never dinner."

He's close now, a smirk playing on his lips. "Forgetting's your talent, huh? Even me?" he whispers, for my ears only, and my pulse dares to skip. I stand my ground, challenging his gaze. He retreats with a chuckle, serving up the roast like he's won some silent victory. "I'll steer clear for the moment."

As we sit down, Saskya makes her entrance, bounding straight into my arms. "Who's a good girl?" I coo, dodging glares.

"Petra, the dog's got rules," Rodrigo's voice cuts in, a hint of steel there. Saskya, traitor to the cause, abandons me for his stern command.

"Lighten up, will you? She's just being friendly. Maybe you should show her some love instead of being a jerk." I say, hoping to get under his skin. Spoiler alert? It works like a charm.

"Love? You wouldn't recognize the word if it bit you."

"Excuse me?" I say.

"You can't even love yourself, let alone a poor animal."

"Um, guys," Deborah interrupts, trying to break the ice. "Can we please not fight at the dinner table?" But I'm locked in battle mode, standing my ground like a fortress against Rodrigo's siege.

"Love?" I scoff, chin up, arms like shields, "I'll have you know that I'm very much capable of loving myself, Saskya, or anyone else. Unlike some people."

Pedro's had enough, his voice a weary buffer. "Give it a rest, you two," he chimes, but he's white noise in the background.

Rodrigo's not done, though. He leans in, all stormy eyes and raw edges. "You are so good at loving yourself that I blink, and you end up in another man's arms – a jerk who ultimately cheated on you if I recall." He says, hitting a nerve.

I'm a live wire, sparking with fury. "Why the hell do you care, Rodrigo?" I snap, fire to his ice. "Does it bother you? Because I'm pretty sure that's none of your damn business."

His anger's a match to mine. "Bothered?" He's almost spitting the words. "More than you know." But then he chokes on the rest, like the truth's too hot to handle.

"What gets to you, Rodrigo?" I prod, daring him to unravel. "Say it."

His face is a thundercloud, inches from mine. "Want the truth?" he growls, a challenge.

The room's holding its breath, Pedro and Deborah frozen spectators.

But I'm done – done with his games, his words, his nearness.

"I'm done with this bullshit. I'm going to bed." I whirl around, storming off, leaving chaos in my wake.

This fucking dinner.

This fucking day.

—

RODRIGO

Pedro tosses me a look that's one part concern, two parts frustration. "What's up with you, man?"

I toss the napkin aside, my appetite fleeing as fast as my patience. "Nothing," I grunt, my eyes narrowing as I stare at Pedro's curious gaze. My fork drops against the plate as I push my food around, and my hunger is gone. "What do you care, anyway?"

"You're asking me why do I care?" Pedro's eyebrows rise, challenging, "Why do YOU care?"

With a huff, I stand, my chair scraping back. A smirk tugs at my lips despite the storm brewing inside. "I don't. I've lost it, along with my appetite." My words are ice, my smile all fire. "Let me spell it out for you, brother. I. Don't. Care. I simply don't give a fuck." But even as I say it, I'm calling for Saskya, needing that golden furball to save me from my own lies.

I snatch my blazer, my retreat planned, when Pedro's voice hooks me back. "It's a real tragedy, you know? You two used to be close. Now? It's like a catfight every time you're in the same room."

I scoff, raking a hand through my hair in frustration. "Close? That's a stretch." And that's the biggest lie of the night.

"Saskya!" I call again, but the dog's vanished like my self-control.

"And bringing up Douglas?" Pedro's not letting up, "What's the point, huh?"

"Just making a damn point," I snap, but the worry for my MIA dog is gnawing at me. "Sask, where are you?"

Pedro shakes his head, disappointment heavy in his voice. "You've never made any sense. She didn't reach out, fine, but you never did either. And I still remember you, calling me from New York, all worked up over a picture of them on Instagram."

I freeze, feeling like a cornered animal, but I refuse to engage. I need to find Saskya.

"They split," Pedro's still talking, "And when I told you, did you care? Not a bit. But years later, here you are, using it just to score a point in an argument?"

I let out a curse, my frustration boiling over. "Pedro, for heaven's sake. Can't you just drop it? I used the info. I'm an ass. Are you satisfied now?"

He's about to say more when, finally, Saskya appears, saving me from another round.

"There you are. What took you so long?" I kneel down, scratching behind her ears, and clip on her leash. "Let's go." I don't look back as we leave the apartment, the door closing with a click.

Settling behind the wheel, guilt crashes into me like a wave. "Damn it," I curse, forehead against the steering wheel. Saskya whines softly, sensing my inner turmoil.

I shouldn't have said what I did to Petra – I shouldn't have picked or joined that fight. I was lying through my teeth when I said I didn't care about her feelings. The truth is like a punch to the gut – I wish I could stop caring, but she means more to me than I can ever admit, even to myself.

—

PETRA

The door crashes against the wall like a gavel, my personal declaration of war against... well, everything. I pace back and forth, my thoughts a whirlwind of 'should-have-saids' and 'next-time-I-wills'. "Rodrigo thinks he can just play puppet master with me?" I spit out to the silence, my voice a serrated knife, cutting through the thick air.

Anger is an old friend, but tonight, it's more like an inferno, scorching everything in its path, and I'm standing smack in the middle. My pulse hammers in my ears, a reminder that I'm this close to boiling over. "Breathe," I tell myself, "Just breathe." But Rodrigo's smug face is branded on the inside of my eyelids, and every breath is gasoline on the fire. "I should've let him have it," I growl, clenching my fists.

It's always the same with him – Rodrigo speaks, and the world bows. Well, not this time. Except, I did walk away, didn't I? He scored, game, set, match, and I... I let him.

The sound of two knocks ricochets around the room, a stark interruption to my self-berating monologue. The door creeps open, and Deborah's there, all soft eyes and tentative smiles. "Mind if I join the pity party?" she half-jokes, but there's concern in her eyes.

Part of me wants to scream 'go away', but that part's a coward, and I'm no coward. "Yeah, come in," I relent, stepping aside, a reluctant host.

She shuffles in, Saskya in tow, trailing like a furry shadow.

Deborah perches on the edge of my bed, her presence a calm in the storm. "So, what was that dinner disaster all about?" her voice is soft as silk.

I let out a sigh that feels like it's been building for years. "I don't know," I admit, but it's a lie. I know alright. It's a tango with Rodrigo – we dance around the truth, two steps forward, one step back.

"You and Rodrigo, it's like watching a soap opera," Deborah says, a hint of a smile playing on her lips. "Except I can't change the channel."

I chuckle despite myself, "Yeah, and he's always trying to be the star of the show."

She leans in, "You know, if you two put as much energy into getting along as you do into these battles, you'd solve world peace."

"Or we'd start World War III."

"Come on, spill," she nudges. "What's really going on in that head of yours?"

I flop down on the bed, "It's ancient history," I huff out to Deborah, all vague and evasive. It's easier that way.

Saskya is caught between loyalty and curiosity, torn as Rodrigo's voice filters through the walls, calling her. She's a four-legged embodiment of my own inner conflict, and it's almost comical. I reach out, scratching behind her ears in a silent apology for the drama.

Deborah's eyes narrow, she's got that look – the one that says she's about to dive deep. "Ancient history, huh?" She arches a brow. "Was there ever, I don't know, more to it? Some kind of... spark?"

I whirl on her, my voice a sharp crack. "No!" It's louder than I intend, a protest too much. "He's just – infuriating. Always barging in like he owns the place, and now my headspace, too."

"But if he's under your skin, there's gotta be a reason, right?" She's relentless. "It was all so rushed when he left. You. Him. The space in between."

Her words hit like a sucker punch, and I'm momentarily winded. "What are you implying?"

"That maybe there's a whole lot of unfinished business there," she says, and damn her, she's not wrong.

Rodrigo's voice rises again, calling Saskya, and I use the distraction to flee the interrogation. I kneel beside Saskya, pulling her into a tight hug. "Go to him," I whisper, and she darts off after one last slobbery kiss, leaving me grounded in my lie of omission.

Deborah's on her feet, her eyebrow doing that thing again, calling out my evasion. "Nice sidestep," she notes, and I can almost hear the smirk in her voice. "Keep your secrets, for now."

I rake a hand through my hair, "I'm not hiding anything," I lie, a little too quickly.

She smiles, all soft edges, "It's cool. I'm here, no judgments. Whenever you're ready."

I nod, my eyes tracing the pattern on the duvet. "I know."

She heads for the door, pausing to wrap me in a quick hug. "Take your time," she says, and then she's gone.

I'm alone with my thoughts again. Eyes closed, I let out a long breath, sinking into the pillows. Today's drama can wait until tomorrow.

CHAPTER SIX

RODRIGO
SIX YEARS AGO

I'm pacing the floor of my room, a one-man circus of internal chaos. "Well, this is a freaking mess," I mutter to myself, throwing a hand through my hair.

It's not just a mess – it's a disaster of epic proportions. How am I supposed to tell her I'm going away? That I'm jetting off to Spain for who-knows-how-many-years? The mere thought has my stomach in knots and my heart pounding like it's trying to break free.

But it's a twister inside me because, damn it, I love her. She's the other half of my best-friend duo, and hell, she's so much more. But life's calling – my career's on the line – and I can't play hooky for love. *Not even for her.*

I'm not the 'long-distance' guy. Hell, I'm barely the 'same-city' guy. I've got the emotional bandwidth of a teaspoon. And yet, the last thing I want to do is hurt her. She's the last person on this godforsaken planet who deserves that. I let the boundaries blur, and that's on me.

So here I am, gearing up to shatter her heart. Because it's the noble thing to do, right? Because ripping the Band-Aid off now is better than the slow peel later.

I'm wrestling with my conscience, trying to prep the speech. Got to tell Petra the truth – about my career, my dreams, the no-space-for-love policy I've got going on. She needs the gentle version, the 'it's not you, it's me' classic.

But what if she fights for us? What if she plays the 'stay' card? Can't let that happen. This is my shot, and I can't miss it for a maybe, for a what-if.

Time's ticking. I'm out of here in weeks. Gotta rip off the veneer, make her believe that what we had was a flash in the pan, just a fling. It's gonna burn, but it's for the best. For both of us.

I snatch my phone, draft the text with a heavy heart. "Hey, can we talk? How about that cafe by the library?" My thumb hovers over 'send.' I'm about to drop a bomb with a side of espresso.

—

I plunk myself down at an outside table of the cafe, my nerves buzzing, but I need to do this. I wait for Petra to show up, drumming my fingers on the table as I try to relax.

She shows up, all sunshine and smiles. Dammit, she's beautiful, and it's like taking a punch to the gut.

I wave at her and gesture to the waiter to bring us some coffee. She slides into the chair across from me, and we stare at each other in awkward silence.

"So," she dives in, all innocent curiosity. "What's the emergency, huh? You look like something's going on."

I release a breath I didn't know I was holding. "We gotta talk about... us," I say, and boy, does it feel like I'm walking a plank. She's all attentive, eyes locked on mine, and that's when I drop the bomb. "It was a mistake," I say, and it's like I've slapped her with my words.

"A mistake?" Her voice is pure confusion and dawning hurt.

"Yeah, us," I push on, feeling like the world's biggest douche. "This – whatever this is."

The coffee arrives, and she thanks the waiter with a smile that doesn't reach her eyes anymore. As he walks away, so does her warmth, and we're back to brewing in silence.

Then she hits me with a bitter chuckle. "So, now you regret it, Rodrigo? Now you want to take it all back? We were friends before, and you—"

I shoot back without thinking. "We were never really friends." *Great, Rodrigo, top-notch asshole material.*

She recoils, looking like I've just handed her a live grenade. "You finally realized that, huh? Or were you just pretending to be nice all this time?"

"That's not what I meant," I stumble over the words, trying to salvage this trainwreck. "Look, I don't do relationships, alright? And I definitely won't keep this one going with you."

She's not having any of it. "You're joking, right? Tell me you're not this spineless."

"I'm dead serious, Petra. I'm going to Spain, and who knows when I'll come back."

Her fuse is lit, and she's a firework about to explode. "Well, good riddance!" She's spitting the words out now. "But let's get one thing straight – you started this circus. You kept the 'friendship' alive – you leaned in for that kiss, you pulled me into this... thing." I can almost see the memories flashing in her eyes, each one a dagger. "And now you're sitting here, handing me this crap about not being capable of a relationship, especially not with me? That we were never even friends?" She's a portrait of scorned fury, and I've painted it. "Was this all some sick joke to you? A last hurrah before you jet off to Spain?" Her voice is laced with venom, and it stings like hell because she's not wrong.

I'm in too deep, and there's no graceful exit. "I suppose you could see it that way," I admit, my guilt trying to choke me.

"Go to hell, Rodrigo," she snaps, and I've never seen something so beautiful look so broken.

I'm watching her, wishing I could rewind and erase, but this is the bed I've made.

"I thought you were different," she says, a storm in her eyes. "But I was a fool. I'm glad you've shown your true colors. You're not worth it. Not worth a damn thing."

She downs her coffee like it's a shot of disdain, grabs her things, and stands up with a glare that could freeze lava.

"Just go to hell," she repeats, coat on like armor, bag in hand like a shield. She doesn't leave before she fires one last parting shot. "I regret ever giving you the time of day."

And then she's gone, leaving me with nothing but the bitter aftertaste of my own stupidity.

Too late, Rodrigo. Way too late.

—

RODRIGO
NOW

I slam my car door shut, welcoming the blissful silence of my garage. Tomorrow's showdown at the office – I'll have to face the mess of merging my dad's company and pretending everything is just peachy with Petra.

No big deal, right? *Wrong*. How did I get myself into this?

Saskya hops out of the car, oblivious to my internal melodrama. We trudge inside, and I flick on the lights and the drama of my reflection hits me. "Get it together, man," I mutter to the guy in the mirror. He looks like he's been chewed up by Wall Street and spat out by Silicon Valley.

Saskya's nails click against the tile as she bolts to her bowl, and I follow, hoping kitchen sounds can drown out my thoughts. Hands washed, I slug back a glass of water like it's whiskey – neat and burning all the way down.

I trudge upstairs, my footsteps heavy with the dread of tomorrow's corporate ballet. I grab sleepwear and head to the shower, craving the scalding cleanse of a day's worth of stress. But even the promise of hot water doesn't wash away the weight on my shoulders. "Nope, can't deal," I groan, aborting the shower mission for a nicotine hit.

Out on the balcony, I spark up a cigarette, the night's chill a slap to my heated skin. The city's quiet, but my mind's a damn rock concert – loud, chaotic, out of control.

Cigarette number two joins the first, ash kissing ash in the tray. I need a distraction, something mindless, so I pull out my phone and thumb over to Instagram. Maybe a scroll through filtered realities can make mine seem less... catastrophic.

Scrolling through my friends' Instagram stories, the only thing I can bring myself to do is scoff. Their perfectly curated lives flash before me – tanned faces, glittering parties, recycled memes. It all feels so hollow. I crave something raw, something that'll shock my heart back into rhythm.

Impulsively, I punch in Petra's name on the search bar — yeah, *I know it's straight out of a cheesy rom-com*. Her profile pops up, a digital gallery of her world travels. There she is, laughing under the Parisian lights, striking a pose in the heart of Rome, lost in the neon sea of Tokyo. Each snapshot a stab of 'what could've been'.

"Why'd it go down in flames?" I mutter, my voice lost to the night. I power off my phone with a sigh that feels like I'm surrendering my soul. "Done with today," I declare to the silence.

In my room, I slam dunk my laundry into the hamper like it's the final seconds of a tied game. Shower, I need that shower. As the water cascades over me, washing away the grime of regret, my phone rings. Pedro's name flashes. What does he want now? Can't a guy get a moment of peace?

I let it ring, the droplets drumming out the disturbance. Shower done, I towel off and face my foggy reflection. Mid-toothbrushing session, Pedro rings again. *Persistent much?* With a mouth full of foam, I pick up. "What?" I growl, the word frothy and annoyed.

Pedro sounds rushed. "Dad's ready to talk about your offer."

I spit out the paste, my interest piqued. "Oh, really?" I say, going hands-free to rinse.

"Yeah. But what are you — brushing your teeth?" Pedro's confusion is almost amusing.

"Bingo," I snap, a little too snappy. "And what's Dad's angle?"

Pedro hesitates, "He wants to tweak some stuff in the company."

My gut twists. "Tweaks like what?"

"He agrees with Petra. He thinks your proposal's solid."

I almost choke on air. "He agrees with who, now?"

"Shit…" he mutters, sounding like he just spilled his coffee.

"What does Petra have to do with anything?"

"Well, after you left the meeting this morning, Dad wanted to talk to someone who knew their stuff about the IP department," Pedro explains. "Since you're trying to get the whole IP team from the company, and Petra is the head of formalities, she was the chosen one. She had no clue we were talking about you, by the way. Dad just asked her what she thought about your offer, never said your name, and she gave him an honest and unbiased answer."

"Petra is head of formalities?" I ask, trying to wrap my head around this new piece of information. *How didn't I know that?*

"Exactly," Pedro confirms.

"And she's against the deal?" I probe, hoping for clarity.

"Nope," Pedro corrects. "She said she would be open to it, depending on the terms."

That's Petra for you — always a thorn in my side, even when she's not trying.

"You still there?" Pedro nudges.

"Yeah, just… processing." I shake off the shock. "So, tomorrow, same place, same time?"

"Yep, just try not to look like you've been in a bar fight this time."

CHAPTER SEVEN

PETRA

"Shit, shit, shit..." Cursing under my breath, I make a break for the office, legs pumping like I'm in the final lap of a 100-meter dash. I'm usually the early bird who gets the worm, always getting prime parking and the first pick of the office donuts. But this morning, the snooze button seduced me into tardiness.

I bust through the office doors, my bag swinging wild enough to take someone's eye out. In my haste, I ricochet off the door as it boomerangs back, clocking me square in the face. "Ow!" I hiss, clutching my possibly broken nose – praying I haven't just shattered a pane of company property because, let's be real, my wallet can't swing that kind of repair.

The office crowd's got front-row seats to my debacle, a few snickers breaking out. I flash a tight-lipped grin, throwing a half-hearted "Mornin'!" into the mix, and book it to my desk. I'm late, like, Cinderella-losing-her-slipper-at-midnight late.

My bag plops onto the desk as I power up my PC.

Bea sidles up, all sunshine and sass, "Hey, hey, hey..."

"Not now, Bea," I fire back, my fingers hammering out my password with the fury of a woman denied her morning buzz. "I'm one skipped latte away from full meltdown. Besides, I need coffee first." I pause, throwing her a look sharp enough to slice. "Trust me, you don't wanna be around for the caffeine crash. It ain't pretty."

Bea throws her hands up, all mock offense. "Alright, alright, keep your hair on. I'll leave you to your coffee hunt," she says before sauntering back to her desk, tossing out grumbles like confetti.

With a sigh, I dive into my purse, finding my phone, and trudge upstairs, eyes glued to the screen. It's on a rebellious streak, refusing to recognize my face. As I'm about to faceplant into my phone, bam – I body slam into Pedro's freshly opened office door. "Not again!" I wail, now nursing a throbbing head and a bruised ego.

"You really need to work on your coordination, Bird," Rodrigo's voice floats down.

Peering up through the haze of my second mishap of the morning, there he is – Rodrigo, looking like a GQ model in his tailored shirt and coat, the epitome of unflappable cool with his hands casually pocketed.

"Maybe you could try not being a human obstacle course?" I shoot back, pressing my phone to my new bump like an ice pack.

"You good?" He's trying for concerned, but I can hear the laughter dancing on the edge of his words.

I shoot Rodrigo a skeptical look. "Oh, I'm sure you're real concerned," I say as I breeze by him, hell-bent on getting my caffeine salvation from the office kitchen.

Stealing a quick glance back, I spot him rooted to the spot, now with Pedro at his side, deep in conversation. Pedro, ever the morning person, catches my eye and beams a sunny 'Good morning, Petty!' which practically has me squinting. I muster a half-hearted wave, drawing Rodrigo's gaze. He gives me a once-over that's slow and speculative, his eyes lingering just a tad too long, stirring something fluttery in my stomach.

I'm jolted back to reality by Mr. Gomez's voice, a teasing lilt to it as he observes the exchange from Pedro's office. "Ms. Smith, capturing the room – and my son's undivided attention – without saying a word. It's a gift, really."

I cough awkwardly, aiming for polite despite the awkwardness. "Morning, Mr. Gomez," I offer, hoping to sound casual enough.

Rodrigo simply pivots his head towards his father, his expression a mastered poker face, before his scrutinizing gaze lands back on me. His face is a cipher, revealing *nada*.

The Gomez men, with their carbon-copy good looks and magnetic pull, always seem to be playing a game of who's the alpha. Pedro's the outlier, Mr. Congeniality with his warm grins and easy charm, while Rodrigo and the senior Gomez are like live wires – charged, compelling, and slightly intimidating with their steely stares and chiseled jaws. They've got this air of strategic mastery, like chess grandmasters in a world of checkers players.

"I better go," I say, cutting through the tension and my own rambling thoughts. "Coffee won't pour itself." I flash them a grin, throwing a daring look at Rodrigo. His response? A subtle lip bite that sets off a ripple of... something, deep down. I tear my eyes away, telling myself to ignore it, ignore him, as I duck into the sanctuary of the kitchen.

—

The clock strikes one and it's lunchtime. I'm plotting trip to Subway when Pedro and Mr. Gomez descend from their offices, all suave and polished. Mr. Gomez lingers while Pedro sidles up to me.

"Petty, we need to talk to you. Do you have any plans for lunchtime?" Pedro asks, his eyes all hopeful puppy dog.

"Subway's calling my name," I admit, already mourning the loss of my footlong dream.

"Join us for lunch instead?" he offers, and there's an ease about him that screams this isn't just about munching on pasta.

"Uh, sure, but is everything okay?"

"Everything is okay, yes." he grins, all charm. "And hey, if having lunch with the big boss man isn't your scene, just tell me. It's fine."

I shrug, game face on. "Lead the way."

Stepping into the Italian joint they pick is a sensory slap – it's like walking into a movie set. Red velvet, chandeliers, the works. The maître d' ushers us to a table that screams 'deal-making' and I'm half expecting a director to yell 'cut'.

Mr. Gomez kicks off the conversation, all gentlemanly apologies for the impromptu lunch, and I'm all grace and smiles, playing it cool.

Then Pedro drops a bomb, casually tossing Rodrigo's name into the mix, "So, Petra, you're here because my dad agreed to Rodrigo's proposal."

"Wait, back up. Rodrigo's what now?" I almost choke on my sparkling water.

The two men exchange a look that's got 'plot twist' written all over it. Yesterday they were talking about merging companies with Rodrigo. *Shoot me now, please.*

"That's right, Ms. Smith," Mr. Gomez confirms, his fingers steepled. "Rodrigo's got grand plans for a merger, and I'm on board. But—" he adds, a glint in his eye, "—no signing without safeguarding my team. That means lockdown contracts for the IP team."

I'm nodding, but my brain's doing somersaults. The waiter sashays over, pouring wine like it's liquid strategy, and I'm trying to keep up.

"Here's the kicker," Mr. Gomez leans in, "Rodrigo wants to be the lawyer in charge of the IP team. However, we have requested that you remain the head of formalities, non-negotiable."

"Did he agree to that?" I ask doubtfully.

"He said he never planned to kick you out as the head of the formalities unit, as he will need someone reliable to lead the legal team while he handles the technical one."

I nearly spit out my wine. Rodrigo, the thorn in my side, thinks I'm reliable now? *That's news.*

"What do you think, Ms. Smith?" Mr. Gomez asks, eyeing me like I'm the last puzzle piece.

"Um, Papá, maybe we should give Petra some time to process this information," Pedro chimes in, "Let's talk cannoli and carbonara before contracts, okay?"

—

RODRIGO
BEFORE LUNCH

My dad leans back, all casual confidence with his leg draped over the other, looking every bit the master negotiator. "So, the deal's this," he starts, fixing me with that steely gaze, "I will only allow your involvement with my Intellectual Property team if they all sign new contracts guaranteeing that they won't leave my company to work for yours in New York."

I nod, "Crystal clear. But here's my play – I'm stepping up to the technical IP team. Who is currently in charge of this team?"

"Right now, there's no one in charge of the technical team. Assigning the processes to one of the team members isn't anyone's particular job. Usually, Dad does it from afar whenever a new case shows up." Pedro pipes up.

I lean in, fixing my gaze on my dad. "Change of plans, then. I want to take over that part of the work from now on. I don't want you–" I say, staring at my dad, "–to have anything to do with any IP work from now on. Is that something you could agree on?"

Dad raises an eyebrow, "What about the formalities team?"

"What about them?" I ask back, "I've heard you already have someone in charge of the formalities team. I don't want to mess with that if that person is doing a good job. I need someone I can trust to help me with the Intellectual Property stuff. I will handle the technical side of the field, and she will handle the formalities."

"Great, it sounds like we're all on the same page here," Pedro says.

Leaning back, I shoot my next question, "Can you tell me more about their work schedules?"

Pedro offers a rundown on the IP team's flexible schedule, mentioning they can start their day anytime between eight and ten in the morning and head out between five and seven in the evening, completing their eight-hour shift with an hour for lunch and no strict rules on coffee breaks.

I nod, absorbing the details. "What about overtime? Is it compensated or banked for later use?"

"They bank it as extra leave," Pedro clarifies.

"And do they often work overtime?"

"It depends," Pedro says, "Tech team members might, since they can work from home. The formalities team usually doesn't, except for Petra. She stays late, off the clock, to get ahead for the next day."

I am baffled. That girl is something else, isn't she?

Dad cuts through my musings, "Do you accept my conditions?"

"Only if you're cool with mine," I shoot back.

"I guess we have a deal then."

I nod, get up, and shake his hand across Pedro's desk, "We have a deal, Mr. Gomez."

As I'm leaving the office, I hear a loud bang after opening the glass door. Petra's cursing under her breath, nursing her head.

"You really need to work on your coordination, Bird," I quip, but I can't hide a brief smirk. She's quick with a fiery comeback. Typical. Yet, I can't resist checking on her. "You good?" I ask. Her reply's laced with sarcasm, and she strides off, leaving me in a chuckle.

Pedro sidles up, whispering, "Smooth talking with the big boss." He's not wrong. I spin around and see Petra is still in the hall, heading to the kitchen door. As Pedro says, "Good morning Petty!" she beams at him with those gorgeous full lips and greets him back. When her eyes meet mine, I realize I am gawking at her. But I don't try to look away.

Dad pipes up, "Ms. Smith, capturing the room – and my son's undivided attention – without saying a word. It's a gift, really."

I bite back my retort, not wanting to tarnish the triumph of our deal.

Petra eventually makes her exit, off for her caffeine fix, and there's a brief lock of eyes – a silent conversation in a glance – before she pivots and vanishes. And just like that, she's all I can think about.

CHAPTER EIGHT

PETRA
NOW

Drowning in an ocean of info-overload, I'm bracing for the tidal wave of more to come. As Mr. Gomez and Pedro start picking appetizers for lunch, I butt in and ask, "Is the team moving to a new place, or are we staying in the building we work at now?"

Mr. Gomez shoots me a look, one eyebrow cocked. "Do you always have the knack for being this... timely, Ms. Smith?" There's a mysterious lilt to his voice, and I'm playing a mental game of 'Nice or Nasty' trying to decode it.

Feeling my cheeks flare up, I'm stuck in a weird limbo of words. Should I respond? Should I stay quiet?

He turns his attention to the waiter bringing our appetizers, thankfully breaking the awkward standoff. "Didn't bring this up with my son," he comments casually, arranging his napkin with unnecessary precision. "You've got a talent for catching the details I miss," he adds, nonchalantly spreading pâté on a tiny toast like it's no big deal. Compliments from Mr. Gomez are as rare as a sunny day in London, and he's never thrown one my way before. So, I'm cashing this in as a win.

"Thanks, Mr. Gomez," I manage, "Means a lot, coming from you."

Mr. Gomez is halfway through turning a toast into an appetizer casualty when he throws me a curveball. "But —" he says with a mouthful, "—if you had to pick, would you stay where you are, or would you rather switch places?"

Honestly, it's not something that I care much about. I'm cool with either, but I am used to the people I work with and where I work. So, I lay it out for him with a smile. "It's not something that bothers me much, really," I say, "I am used to the place I work and the people around me, but if I have to go to the other site, I will adjust. As long as I have my computer and a steady supply of coffee, I can work from anywhere."

Mr. Gomez chews on that thought, then speculates, "My bet's on Rodrigo wanting the IP team to go hybrid." He turns to Pedro, "Your take, hijo?"

"We all know Rodrigo is pretty unpredictable, Papá," Pedro says.

And let me tell you, Rodrigo's unpredictability is like trying to guess the next twist in a soap opera. It's like Seattle weather in human form — one minute it's all sunshine and rainbows, the next, it's a downpour of pure chaos.

I'm jolted back to planet Earth when Pedro drops this gem, "But yeah, I'd put my money on Rodrigo pushing for the IP team to go hybrid. It's all about the workload and the technical focus in the projects."

Interrupting with a casual flair, I set down my wine glass — after a strategic sip, of course. "Hold up," I say. "Why does the technical focus matter here? How would it affect working hybrid or not?"

Pedro leans in like he's sharing state secrets. "Here's the thing. Rodrigo's kinda obsessed with being hands-on in trademark and patent oppositions, and we have a ton of opposition cases on our plate, especially trademarks. In his company in New York, he was always the one who went to court for the appeals, even though he had a whole legion of lawyers working with him."

And here's the kicker – I'm the one pulling the strings behind all those trademark showdowns. Which means Rodrigo and I are about to get up close and uncomfortably personal in the work ring. *Oh, the realization hits me like a bad sitcom plot*. Welcome to the world of awkward office air.

But hey, we're adults, right? We can totally handle a bit of workplace drama. Just gotta keep it strictly professional.

Easy peasy – famous last words.

—

RODRIGO

What a week. If my life was a TV show, this episode would be called 'The Disaster Diaries.' It's like a tornado waltzed through my days, doing the cha-cha with my sanity.

First off, I had to fly back from New York like some big shot, which was a trip in itself. Then I had to sort everything out and catch up on a zillion things, all while bumping into Petra – who, by the way, has been giving me the cold shoulder and some very frosty looks ever since I first saw her again. Oh, and let's not forget the little issue of sealing the merger deal with my dear old dad.

I'm pretty sure this circus is shaving years off my life. But hey, it's the weekend, right? Wrong. Technically it is Friday night alright, but there's still a whole lot of ways for things to go wrong.

I've just kicked off my shoes, about to embrace the sweet, sweet couch, when my phone – which has about as much life left in it as a zombie in a horror movie – rings. And who else but Sofia?

"Yo," I answer, aiming for record time in ending this call. "Heads up, I'm on my last phone-life percent here."

She's like, "Aren't you home?"

"And your point is?"

She rolls out the sarcasm. "Ever heard of a charger? It's this magical device–"

"Yeah, yeah, thanks for the tech support," I cut in. "Didn't realize my baby sis was all grown up, schooling her big bro."

She's already winding up for a fastball. "Cut the crap. Tomorrow, you're taking me shopping. No debates."

"Hilarious, really."

"Your demon spawn of a pet shredded my beautiful dress, remember? You're buying me a new one, as per the brother-sister peace treaty."

"Whoa, hold up, Piglet," I tease, just to push her buttons. "I don't remember signing up for a shopping marathon. I've got better things to do."

She's mid-rant when – perfect timing – my phone decides to play Sleeping Beauty. I grin and toss my phone on the couch.

Striding into the living room, I step down into my chill zone, neatly sidestepping the couch that's strategically placed as a visual shield from the front door. I debate about plugging in my phone, but nah, let's embrace the sweet sound of silence. Sure, the never-ending symphony of work calls is music to my ears, but sometimes, you just need a break from the orchestra.

I make a dash for the couch, in a mini-Olympics race against Saskya for the TV remote. And guess who's winning? The furry tornado. She's already got it, treating it like her personal chew toy. Great. I dive into a tug-of-war with her, muttering every sailor's curse I know.

Victory is mine, but the remote's looking like it survived a shark attack — all slobbered up and decorated with teeth marks. I flop down on the couch, switching on the TV, feeling like I've run a marathon. Saskya, mission accomplished, trots off in search of her next victim, leaving a crime scene of fur and drool.

So much for peace and quiet. I haul myself up, off the couch, on a quest for some elusive tranquility.

—

PETRA

"Dee, come on, cut me some slack!" I whine, pulling out the world's saddest puppy dog eyes. "This week chewed me up and spat me out. I'm practically a zombie." I'm playing my last card here, hoping Dee's got a hidden stash of sympathy somewhere. A girl can dream, right? But Dee? She's always got a plan that's 100% Dee-certified, and chilling isn't usually on the menu.

"Not happening!" Dee plants her hands on her hips like she's about to lay down the law. "It's Friday night, for fuck's sake. You're not turning into a couch potato on my watch. What are you, 90?"

"I swear I aged a decade just last night," I say, laying it on thick with the sad eyes.

Dee's having none of it. She grabs my arm, practically yanking me off my feet. "You're coming to the mall with me. Pedro's birthday is coming up, and I need a present and something snazzy to wear. And don't you dare start with your excuses."

"But, but..." I sputter, my brain scrambling for an escape plan. "His birthday isn't until next week. We've got ages!"

Dee's eyes roll so hard I'm worried they might get stuck. "As if we're gonna have time next week. Plus, you're being a total party pooper tonight. I can't count on you to get out of bed for the rest of the weekend. So, we're going. Now."

"I don't need a new outfit," I try, one last feeble attempt at freedom.

"Yes, you do," she shoots back, eyeing my current getup like it's a fashion crime scene. "And don't even think about showing up in office gear."

"What's wrong with my clothes?" I protest.

"Nothing," she sighs, in that 'I'm-trying-to-be-patient' way. "But you need a dress. A fresh one."

"I have dresses," I point out.

Dee's patience is wearing thin. "Don't be such a baby," she practically growls. "You need a NEW one. And fine, it can be black," she adds.

She knows me too well, and I can already tell – I'm totally doomed.

I let out a dramatic groan, waving the white flag. "Alright, to the mall we go," I surrender.

Dragging myself to the garage, I'm pretty much zombie-meets-fashion-victim. But the second I plop into Deborah's Fiat 500, which is more cream puff than car, I kiss any dreams of snoozing goodbye. She fires up the engine, and we're zooming out faster than a getaway car in a heist movie.

The drive is like being trapped in a pop music purgatory. I'm trying to play dead, hoping for a quick nap, but Deborah's got other ideas. She cranks the volume to 'ear-bleed' and starts belting out tunes like she's auditioning for talents show.

As we drive, the rain decides to join the party, pelting down like it's got a personal vendetta. But Deborah? She's in her own world, jamming like there's no tomorrow. Despite my exhaustion, I have to crack a smile at her enthusiasm.

We hit the mall, and she parks the car like she's landing a plane on a crowded runway. We escalate our way into the shopping battlefield, me yawning like there's no tomorrow.

Seeing me more dead than alive, Deborah plays good cop and drags me to Starbucks. One industrial-strength coffee later, I'm caffeinated enough to face the shopping apocalypse. And by apocalypse, I mean a whirlwind tour of every store in a three-mile radius.

We're dress-trying-on machines, leaving a wake of rejected fabrics in our path. Finally, I find this killer black mini dress, complete with lace-up booties that mean business. Deborah scores too – a dark blue number that screams 'look at me.' It's like the dress and her were made for each other.

But this fashion safari isn't just about upgrading our wardrobes. She's on a mission for Pedro's present and nails it with a watch so flashy, it could blind.

All in all, it's been a pretty good shopping trip.

CHAPTER NINE

Here I am, propped up against the cinema's chilly wall, waiting on Deborah and Pedro. It's ticking past nine, and the cinema's neon sign is doing this flashy dance thing overhead.

"Think they're gonna show?" I murmur, phone in hand, hope dwindling by the second.

Ping! It's Deborah, "Hey, sorry, things got... interesting with Pedro. Won't make it tonight. Have fun!"

I burst out laughing, showing Rodrigo the text. He lets out this deep, hearty laugh, eyes crinkling. "Looks like we're not the only ones with a horror show tonight," he quips.

Screw it, we dive into the movie anyway. It's one of those exorcism flicks where the plot's thinner than a ghost.

We slide into our seats in the almost-too-cool darkness of the cinema, the screen lighting up and casting eerie shadows around us. I steal a look at Rodrigo, lounging in his seat like he owns the place, one arm thrown casually over the back. He's got this 'too cool for school' vibe that just works, even in a nearly empty, dim cinema.

Rodrigo catches me looking and smirks, "Enjoying the view?"

"Just assessing the cinema's seating arrangements."

He chuckles, "Well, feel free to give it a five-star rating. I'm all about comfort."

I shake my head, laughing softly. The movie starts, and we turn our attention to the screen.

I'm fumbling with the popcorn, the rich, buttery smell making my mouth water. Every time Rodrigo dips his hand in for a few kernels, our fingers brush, sending these ridiculous, fizzy sparks up my arm. *It's ridiculous, really*. It's just popcorn, but with Rodrigo? It's like every little thing is amplified.

The movie kicks into high gear with all the classic horror tropes – squeaky doors, shadows lurking just out of sight. I inch a bit closer to Rodrigo, not because I'm freaked out or anything. It's just... he's got this comforting vibe that's hard to resist. He clocks my move and gives me this knowing smirk, that mischievous glint in his eye.

"Getting scared?" he teases.

I snort, "As if. I'm just ensuring prime popcorn access."

He chuckles, that deep sound that seems to vibrate right through me. "Right, it's all about the popcorn strategy. Of course."

I can't help but grin, even as I roll my eyes. My focus shifts back to the movie, where the characters are about to do something insanely stupid. "Seriously, who goes investigating spooky sounds in a haunted house?" I mutter under my breath.

Rodrigo leans in, his voice low and teasing, his breath warm against my ear. "Probably the same kind of person who thinks chanting from an old Latin book is a good idea," he whispers back, chuckling.

I sneak another glance at him – his face lit by the flickering movie screen, looking every bit like a guy straight out of a movie himself.

The movie's rolling on with its predictable plot and cheesy effects, but honestly, I'm more caught up in the real-life scene next to me. Rodrigo, with his quick wit and that comfortable way he has about him, turns an ordinary movie night into something kind of extraordinary. The movie? Totally forgettable. The night with Rodrigo? Anything but.

Post-movie, we're strolling, the cool night air a welcome change.

"Who even does that? Who checks out the creepy basement?!"

Rodrigo's grinning, "Yeah, like 'Oh, a demon's chilling downstairs, let's say hi'."

"And then they act all shocked when they end up possessed!" I joke, "Seriously, it's like sending a welcome mat to the underworld."

Rodrigo's laugh is infectious, and he leans in, a twinkle in his eye. "It's as if they've never seen a horror movie. Rule number one: weird noises are a no-go zone!"

I nod, "Never go solo! Did they skip every horror movie ever? Stay in a group! Basic survival 101."

"Exactly! And if your walls suddenly turn into a Jackson Pollock painting with blood, maybe it's time to Airbnb somewhere else?" he suggests, still chuckling.

I crack up at that. "Oh, and let's not forget the classic spooky book covered in dust and doom. If I found that, I'm not reading it. I'm hitting up a cleaning service!"

"Right?!" Rodrigo joins in the laughter. "And then there's the 'I'm sure if we ignore it, it'll just go away' approach."

"Which always works out perfectly, doesn't it?" I say sarcastically. "I mean, if you're going to chant Latin from a book that looks like it belongs to Dracula, you're just asking for trouble."

"We should make a 'Horror Movie Survival Guide.' Might save a few lives in these films."

"Sounds like a plan," I agree, grinning back at him. "But for tonight, let's steer clear of any dark basements or spooky spellbooks, deal?"

"Deal," Rodrigo says, giving me a mock salute. "No demon meetups for us. We're all about that ghost-free life!"

Then, classic Petra moment – I nail my knee against a light pole. "Ouch!" I yelp, a weird mix of laughter and pain. Because, honestly, if you don't laugh at yourself, you're missing out on some prime comedy.

Rodrigo's by my side in an instant, his eyes wide with concern. "You good?"

He crouches down, eyeing my knee which is now sporting a lovely shade of 'bruise red.'

"It's just a flesh wound," I jest, doing my best to downplay the throbbing pain.

"Of course, only you could turn a walk into a battle with inanimate objects," he teases.

I stop for a second and then decide to reach out, pulling him into a clumsy, one-legged hug. "Thanks for not ditching me, even though I'm a walking disaster."

He wraps his arms around me, a gentle, sturdy presence. "Not a chance, Bird," he murmurs. "Who else is going to protect you from the dangers of everyday street furniture?"

Bird.

I laugh and we just stand here, huddled together on the sidewalk. And I'm hit with this wave of warmth that has nothing to do with my bruised knee.

—

Okay, so here I am, sprawled on my own couch in my own Caleb-free zone – thank goodness – with Rodrigo by my side. After the whole cinema saga – you know, the knee-meets-light-pole classic Petra move – we figured it'd be safer, and frankly cozier, to just chill at my place. Because apparently, the universe has decided I'm too klutzy for public outings tonight.

We're sprawled on the couch, some Netflix flick murmuring in the background, totally ignored. Rodrigo's got his arm slung around me, and I'm acutely aware of every point where our bodies touch, like little sparks waiting to ignite.

He shoots me this look, you know, the kind that says more than words ever could. "So, Petra," he drawls, "What's the big plan for the night?"

I toss him a playful smirk. "Thought we'd dive into an exciting documentary. Penguins, ever heard of them?"

He laughs, and it's like music, all deep and rich. "Penguins, right. That's some nice stuff."

I'm all ready to throw some witty comment at Rodrigo, but the guy's faster than lightning. Before I can even get a word out, he's right here, closing that tiny gap between us. His lips find mine, and *bam*! It's like we've just stepped into our own little bubble, away from the rest of the world.

The kiss kicks off soft and sweet, kinda like he's testing the waters. *But oh boy, does it shift gears fast.* We're talking zero to a hundred in a heartbeat. It's like a spark turning into a blazing fire, all fierce and full of heat.

I'm leaning into him, hands tracing the muscles on his back, feeling him respond to every touch. Our breaths mingle, charged with an energy that's all about us, here and now.

He breaks away, but only to trace a path with his lips down my neck. I tilt my head back, lost in the sensation, feeling his hands venture under my shirt, his fingertips setting off fireworks along my spine.

"Petra," he breathes out, his voice a tantalizing blend of craving and something else..

Our eyes lock, and it's like the room's temperature just cranked up a few notches. His hands are everywhere, tracing lines of fire across my skin, each touch leaving me wanting more. I can feel every beat of my heart, every breath I take.

As my fingers dance through Rodrigo's hair, a gentle tug pulls a low growl from him, a sound that sends delicious shivers racing down my back.

Rodrigo, ever the man of action, scoops me up effortlessly. My legs wrap around his waist instinctively, feeling right at home there. His hands, strong and confident, grip my butt, a bold move that keeps me pressed against him as we navigate through the house. Our lips remain locked in an avid kiss, each step he takes intensifying the moment.

We reach my room, a sanctuary of sorts, and he gently eases onto the bed without letting me go. The kiss breaks for just a moment, just long enough for me to shed my top, revealing the black bra underneath. Rodrigo's eyes drink me in, a combination of admiration and longing in his gaze. It's a look that says more than words ever could.

He leans in, his lips tracing a tantalizing path from my chest back up to my lips, rekindling the kiss with eagerness. It's my turn now, my fingers fumbling with his shirt, eager to feel the warmth of his skin. The shirt comes off, and there we are, bared to each other in more ways than one.

As I guide us down onto the bed, our bodies meld together perfectly. His skin against mine is like the missing piece of a puzzle I didn't even know was incomplete. Each touch, each caress, ignites a deeper, more intense craving within us. Lying atop him, I feel the steady rhythm of his heart, a beat that seems to echo my own.

Our eyes lock, and in that moment, there's a raw honesty that transcends mere physical attraction.

—

RODRIGO

Waking up in Petra's bed, with the morning sun sneaking through the curtains, feels unreal. Last night was like a dream, except it was real, every moment of it.

I grab my phone, heart skipping a beat at messages from Pedro. "We need to talk about last night." *That's not good.*

I type back a casual "About what?"

He's all, "Meet me at home, lunch." Great, cryptic messages first thing in the morning.

I lock the phone, turning to Petra. She's still asleep, all peace and beauty. I lean over, kiss her cheek gently, trying not to wake her as I get dressed.

She wakes up just as I'm almost done. "Running away from the scene?" she mumbles, all sleepy and cute.

I smile, sit by her. "Would never," I say, giving her a soft kiss. It's a quiet promise, different from last night but just as intense. "I've got to meet Pedro for lunch. He's got something up his sleeve," I tell her.

She checks her phone, surprised. "It's already 11 a.m.? Time does fly."

I nod, getting up. "Especially with you." I leave with one last look. "I'll see you later?" I ask, lingering at the doorway.

She stretches, a smile playing on her lips. "Definitely. Maybe no more horror movies, though?" Her voice is teasing, light.

I chuckle, "Deal. We'll stick to comedies or something less... jump-scarey."

She laughs, and it's like music, "Comedies it is. But I expect popcorn."

"Popcorn, and maybe some of that terrible candy you like," I say, winking.

Her mock indignation is adorable. "Hey, my candy choices are impeccable, thank you very much."

I laugh again, stepping out of the room. "Impeccable and sugary. See you tonight, Bird."

———

I'm sitting across from Pedro at this outdoor restaurant, the kind of place that's casual but tries to look fancier than it is. We've got these oversized umbrellas shielding us from the midday sun, and I'm fidgeting with my glass. The whole time, I'm thinking, *does he know about me and Petra?*

"So, what's up? You said we needed to talk about last night," I start, trying to sound calm.

Pedro takes a sip of his drink, looking surprisingly serious. "Yeah, about last night..."

Here it comes. I brace myself, ready for him to drop some bomb about me not coming home last night.

"Deborah and I, we made a decision. We're moving in together," he blurts out.

I blink, thrown off. "Wait, what? Just like that?"

He nods, a goofy smile spreading across his face. "Yeah, man. It just feels right, you know? I mean, I know it's only been six months, but everything with her just clicks."

I chuckle, shaking my head. "How do you make a decision like that in one night?"

Pedro shrugs, looking more relaxed now. "I don't know, Rodrigo. When it's right, it's right. It's like everything just falls into place. You don't question it; you just go with it."

I lean back, letting his words sink in. It's crazy, moving in together after just six months. But then again, looking at Pedro, seeing how genuinely happy he is, I'm just happy for him.

"So, you guys are serious about this? Moving in together and everything?"

"Yeah, we are. I mean, why wait, right? Life's too short to not take chances," he says, and he's not wrong.

I nod and raise my glass to him, a smile forming. "Well, cheers to taking chances, then."

Pedro clinks his glass against mine, his grin infectious. "To taking chances."

And as we sit here talking about plans, part of my mind is still with Petra. Maybe Pedro's got a point. Maybe sometimes, you've just got to go with what feels right. And

right now, everything about Petra feels righter than
anything I've known.

CHAPTER TEN

My doorbell is ringing. What the hell? It's Saturday — who the fuck shows up at my people's door on a Saturday morning? Ever heard of texting? A little warning would've been nice.

I reach for my phone, ready to give a piece of my mind, but oh, great — it's dead. I totally forgot I had to charge it last night. So maybe, just maybe, this person outside tried calling first. Now they're assaulting my doorbell, turning it into the world's most annoying wake-up call.

I throw on a t-shirt and bolt downstairs, the doorbell still wailing like a siren. I yank the door open, and boom — it's Sofia. What now?

"What do you want?" I grumble, half asleep. "Ever heard of weekends? They're for sleeping, you know."

Sofia's making a face, "Gross, dude. Put on some pants. You're giving me nightmares."

"Hey, you're the surprise guest here," I fire back. "So technically, my boxer show is on you."

Saskya's jumping around Sofia like she's either her new best friend or her next chew toy. "Control your beast," Sofia complains.

Taking a deep breath, I tug Saskya back. I spin around, leaving the door wide open – hint hint, Sofia.

"Suit up," she bosses. "Shopping, now."

I groan. "Not this song and dance again. I told you, no."

She's like a brick wall. "Don't care. Get dressed."

I'm desperate. "I'll pay you," I blurt out. "Just leave."

She perks up. "For the dress?"

"For my peace and quiet," I snap. "I'll pay you to leave me alone."

"But I don't wanna shop solo," she whines.

"Got no friends to bug?"

Her smile's so fake it hurts. "Ha-ha. I do, but I'm not waking them up on a Saturday."

"Except me, right?" I retort. "Thanks for the ruined sleep."

"You think I wanna be here?" she shoots back. "Your dog's a dress destroyer. You owe me."

"Hey, let's be clear," I argue. "You came uninvited." Then it hits me. "I've got it!"

Sofia looks skeptical. "Your ideas usually suck."

"Deborah. She's like a shopping ninja. How about her? Just wait and see," I assure her. "Deborah will be over the moon to shop with you."

"So, you're gonna call her?" Sofia raises an eyebrow, all skeptical. "With your phone that's as alive as a doornail?" She crosses her arms, shooting me a glare that could freeze lava.

It's funny, sometimes I wonder if we're actually related. She's got this whole light hair, skin, and eyes thing going on, totally different from Pedro and me. But then she opens her mouth, and bam, there's no doubt – we're cut from the same cloth.

"Alright, Ms. Smarty-Pants, you call her," I concede with a smirk. "Deborah will be jumping for joy to go mall-crawling with you. Just remember to tell her I said hi."

I'm halfway up the stairs, dreaming of my bed, when Sofia's voice stops me dead.

"Hold up! Where do you think you're going?"

"Back to dreamland," I shoot back.

"No way, Jose," she retorts. "You're driving me to Pedro and Deborah's."

I spin around, exasperated. "You are here and you totally killed my sweet dream, so, how'd you even get here? Just call a cab."

"Uber, duh. What, you want me to hail a cab? What year do you think this is?" she scoffs.

"Then Uber it again!"

"Nope," she's firm as a rock. "You owe me a dress. The least you can do is chauffeur me."

Groaning, I head back to my room to throw on some clothes. "Just call her, alright?"

I'm quick about it – black pants, black polo, and my go-to black and white striped Vans. Down in the garage, Sofia's waiting, and off we go to Deborah and Pedro's.

When we get there, Sofia and Deborah are hugging like long-lost friends. Way too chipper for a Saturday morning.

"What's with the happy faces?" I ask, bewildered by their energy levels.

Pedro appears out of nowhere. "And Deborah hit the mall last night with Petra."

I shake my head in disbelief. "Dee, you're a shopping machine." I hand Sofia a wad of cash, more than enough. "Now shoo, go buy your dress."

Sofia sticks out her tongue and dashes off with Deborah.

"Wanna crash here?" Pedro asks, "You look pretty wiped out. Just go lie down on the couch and take a nap while I go for a run."

I nod. "Sounds like heaven. And I sort of miss running." I say, remembering my daily running routine in New York.

He claps me on the shoulder, all brotherly. "You'll get back into your New York groove, man. You're like a hamster on a wheel — just need a little time."

I collapse on the couch, a heap of tiredness. Sleep's calling my name, and I don't put up a fight. In seconds, I'm out like a light.

—

PETRA

I blink awake, stretching like a cat, with the morning sun playing peek-a-boo through the blinds. I'm already rocking my fuzzy slippers — talk about preparedness. Shuffling out of bed in my cozy-as-a-cloud pajama set — we're talking fuzzy cream shorts and a matching tank top — I head towards the kitchen. Yawning like it's my job, I make a beeline for the coffee pot. It's my morning savior.

"Damn, my phone," I mutter, half-awake.

I backtrack to my room, finding my phone and shoving it into my shorts pocket. *Mission accomplished.*

I'm practically dreaming of that first sip of coffee — black as my soul, no sugar, no milk. Just as I'm pouring the heavenly brew, something catches my eye.

Rodrigo. Out cold on the couch. What in the world?

I pause, coffee mug in hand, staring at him. There he is, all curled up like a teenager after a night out, coat still on, sneakers and all. Funny thing is, since he's been back from New York, I've never seen him in anything but dress shoes. Guess we're both slaves to the dress code at work – no casual Friday for us.

I can't help but smile at the sight of him. There he is, Mr. Hotshot Lawyer, looking all young and carefree, snoozing away like a regular person. Not his couch, but hey, who's counting?

"If you snap a pic, it'll last longer, Bird," Rodrigo quips, eyes still shut, a cocky grin playing on his lips. "Then you can ogle me all you want, on your time."

Busted. I avert my gaze, trying to play it cool. "Wasn't ogling," I mutter, my cheeks burning up. "Just...admiring your snoring skills."

Rodrigo chuckles, eyes flicking open, teasing glint in full effect. "Admiring my snoring, eh? It's a talent. Years in the making." He's still lounging there, eyeing me over as I clutch my coffee like a lifeline. "Got any more of that? Could use a cup to wake up."

I arch an eyebrow. "Pretty sure you're capable of brewing your own. So, if you're fishing for room service, sorry, we're fresh out." I toss him a mischievous smile.

Rodrigo groans, sitting up, rubbing his eyes. "So much for the warm welcome, Bird."

"Drop the nickname, will you?"

"What, 'Bird'?" He shoots me a cheeky smirk. "It suits you. Clumsy little bird."

I spin around, all huffy. "That, Rodrigo, is exactly why you're in the no-love zone." I toss over my shoulder.

"Oh, so it's just the nickname? Really?" I spin back to face him, arms folded like armor. "That's not the real issue. C'mon, we both know what's up." He steps closer, and I'm forced to look up, his breath a tantalizing torment.

My voice is steel, but my heart... it's another story. "Enlighten me, Rodrigo. What do we 'both know'?"

His eyes soften as he leans in, our faces mere inches apart. "You're afraid. Afraid of letting me in again." His eyes flicker to my lips, lingering.

"You're delusional, Rodrigo."

"Am I, though?" His voice is a low rumble, stirring something within me.

"The reason is – you're not worth the effort." I blurt, trying to sound firm.

He arches an eyebrow, unimpressed. "You sure about that?"

"Absolutely." I take a defiant sip of my coffee, trying to mask the chaos inside with a wink.

"Hmm," he hums, hands sliding into his pockets, a knowing look in his eyes.

"'Hmm', what?"

Rodrigo inches closer, his lips dangerously close to mine. "Hmm, as in you're a terrible liar, Bird," he murmurs, a sultry note in his voice.

I feel a flutter in my stomach but stand my ground, "Keep dreaming," I quip with a wink, stepping back.

He changes tack, his tone light, teasing. "So, about your future... Excited to be graced with my presence every day? Must be like winning the lottery."

"Oh, joy. Who wouldn't want a daily dose of the Rodrigo ego trip."

He smirks, undeterred. "Not like you've got better options, right?"

"I've got a waiting list, trust me. You're just not on it," I snap back.

He feigns a daydream, eyes twinkling mischievously. "Picture this: every morning, you, me, and a cup of coffee. You come to my office, close the door, and—"

"Nope, not happening," I interrupt. "And I'm not your personal barista, just so we're clear."

"Shame," he grins wickedly. "You'd probably spill it all over me anyway."

"Please. I've got more important things than ruining your precious wardrobe." I throw him a fake sweet smile, patting his shoulder as I pass.

He's quick to retort, voice dripping with mock awe. "Look at that, physical contact in my brother's kitchen. Imagine the possibilities in my office." His grin's devilish, eyes alight with teasing. He leans in, whispering, his breath tickling my ear. "Maybe I should lock the door and..."

"You'd be lucky to get a glance from me in the office, sweetheart." I push him back. "You really are impossible, you know?"

"But we've got pet names, Bird," he smirks, inching closer again. "See? We're practically an old married couple."

Trying to maintain my composure, I focus on washing my mug, feeling the heat of his gaze on my back. "Were you born this obnoxious, or is it a special skill you've honed over the years?"

He leans against the counter, all casual charm. "Just the right amount to sweep you off your feet once, wasn't it?"

I ignore his comment and walk past him to the couch, pretending to be engrossed in my phone.

Like a shadow, Rodrigo follows and flops down beside me, making the couch dip under his weight. He stretches lazily. "Thought you were gonna make me stand all morning,"

If I ignore him he'll get bored and go away.

"So, Bird," he starts, which means my technique didn't work. "Are you coming to Pedro's birthday dinner?" he prods, lounging back with a grin, "I know it's not every day that you get to celebrate someone's birthday with me, so I figured you wouldn't want to miss it."

"Feeling extra full of yourself today, huh?" I ask, not looking at him. "And what's with this sudden chatty streak? You've been Mr. Silent since coming back from New York."

He frowns, his tone shifting. "Can't a guy be friendly without being a suspect?" The charm fades. "But you're right. Why bother being nice to someone who clearly doesn't want it?" He stands up, the playful Rodrigo replaced by the distant, moody version. "I'm your boss now, remember? Let's keep it professional."

As he heads for the door, back to his brooding New York self, something inside me snaps.

"I'll be there," I blurt out, not daring to look at him. I'm not sure why I say it, but I want him to know.

He pauses, half-turned. "You'll be where?"

"At the dinner," I say, eyes still on my phone. I can't face his reaction, whether it's annoyance or something else.

He hesitates at the door, his tone flat. "Good for you," he says and leaves. The apartment falls silent, leaving me alone with my racing thoughts.

CHAPTER ELEVEN

RODRIGO

What the hell is wrong with me? This fucking weird sensation in my chest. Since when did Rodrigo become such a sentimental sap? *Come on, man, get a grip!*

I'm about to leave, shaking my head to clear it, but Petra's voice stops me cold. "I'll be there," she says, not meeting my gaze.

"You'll be where?" I spin around.

"At the dinner," she mumbles, lips caught between her teeth.

"Hmm," I mutter, swinging the door open. "Good for you." I step out, leaving her behind.

Petra's like this puzzle I can't solve. I keep building walls, but part of me wants to tear them down. To be the guy who used to make her laugh, who'd kiss her so softly, who'd hold her close. But that guy? He's long gone. And she knows it. She saw the change in me before I left for Spain – the cold, distant version of me, avoiding her gaze, her touch, her questions.

Waking up on that couch today, though, seeing her squint at me in her cute pajamas, I lost myself for a moment. All the drama between us just vanished. There she was, still Petra, maybe sassier, with her stunning brown hair, that infectious smile, and that fire in her eyes. She was the same, but I... I'm different. Or at least, I thought I was until she made me forget everything with her simple presence.

I thought I could handle seeing her again. Keep my cool, no big deal. But who was I kidding? I lost my cool the moment I laid eyes on her. There's something about trying to get a rise out of her that's just so damn thrilling.

Seeing Petra again, working with her - it wasn't part of my plan. I came back for business, not to dig up old wounds or face the mess I left behind. But now, she's tied to it all. She's part of the business deal I can't escape.

I'm caught in this crazy situation. I need her expertise for the business, but being around her is playing havoc with my sanity. I'm stuck between needing her close and needing to keep my distance.

Life is funny, full of surprises. And boy, did I get a big one when I ended up doing business with my dad. Three years ago, I was in the Big Apple, launching my own company with a fiery goal – to drive Daddy Dearest's empire into the ground.

I can hear it now, 'Jeez, you're a piece of shit, aren't you?' Yeah, well, Father of the Year he was not. The guy was a walking, talking business manual, sure, but as a dad? Cold as an ice cube, distant like the stars, and demanding like a drill sergeant. Let's just say, I never really felt like I made the grade in his eyes.

Pops and I? Constant head-butting, never seeing eye to eye. Guess the apple didn't fall far from the tree – I got his stubborn streak and that relentless drive. But unlike him, I've got a heart, not just a spreadsheet for a soul.

Pedro though, he's another story. He took the path of least resistance – cozying up to Dad and joining the family business. Me? I bolted to Spain, our old stomping grounds, then hightailed it to New York, where Mom's from. Dad was fuming, thought I betrayed him or something when I set up my own company.

But believe it or not, once upon a time, Little Rodrigo, the mini mogul, that was me. Always tugging at Dad's sleeve, begging to be part of his corporate world. But that was before he turned into Mr. Hyde. Before the endless arguments with Mom, before he broke her heart over and over with his... flings.

Pedro doesn't see it like I do. Either he's got selective memory, or he's the forgiving type. And Sofia? She's blissfully clueless. She knows the 'rents split, but that's it. She missed the whole show – the fights, Mom's tears. For her, Dad's Mr. Perfect, the 'little princess' treatment and all. I'm not gonna lie, there's a part of me that's jealous of that. Deep down, there's this little voice wishing I had that kind of bond with him. But hey, that's life – a mixed bag of nuts, and I got the short straw.

—

PETRA

Midweek blues, and it's business as usual, sort of. Except, Mr. Gomez is MIA, and now Pedro's playing boss man again. Every half hour, Avery's buzzing around him like a busy bee, with papers and phone calls from clients. Rodrigo? That guy's practically a ghost. After his grand exit on Saturday, he's been AWOL. It's like he's vanished off the face of the earth.

Bea sneaks up behind me, nearly giving me a heart attack. "Psst, you hear the latest office gossip?" she whispers, all wide-eyed and conspiratorial.

I jump a mile high. "What gossip?"

"The big one – our company's been sold off to some corporate giant," she murmurs, eyes glinting with excitement.

I shake my head. "Nah, that's a load of bullshit."

Her face falls a bit, and her voice gets a pitch higher. "Really? Tell me everything you know!"

Bea's a living, breathing ray of sunshine, always on a natural high. The woman doesn't even touch coffee – it's herbal tea all the way. It's like she's from another planet.

"Shh, lower your voice!" I hiss.

"Oops, my bad." She clamps her hand over her mouth, looking guiltier than a kid caught with their hand in the cookie jar.

I lean in closer. "Look, what's happening is more like our IP teams – formal and technical – have been... rented out. Kind of like a fancy car."

Her eyes go wide as saucers. "What?! Who's driving us now?"

I glance at her, trying not to roll my eyes. "Chill. We're still part of the same company. And I can't just go blabbing about this, you know? If you're that curious, ask Pedro."

Bea makes a face like she's just bitten into a lemon. "Ew, no way! I can't just march up to Pedro and ask him that. He's the boss, not my buddy."

"Exactly," I nod. "As your boss, he's the one who should explain to you what's going on with your job. You're part of the formal team too, remember? You deal with patents, and I deal with trademarks. We're in the same boat, just rowing with different oars."

Bea huffs, arms crossed. "You're such a buzzkill."

"Don't pull that sad puppy face on me." Locking my computer, I stand up. "Fine, I'll go talk to Pedro. See if he can clear up this mess."

I knock on the glass door of Pedro's office and go inside. He's on the phone, but waves me in. I slump into the chair across from him, waiting for him to finish his call.

"What's up?" Pedro finally asks.

"I'm tired of Bea nagging me about the company being sold. She thinks I know something because I'm close to you. Maybe you should just tell everyone what's going on, or at least give them a hint."

He raises his eyebrows. "Are you serious? Do they really think the company is being sold? Like, for real?" he asks. "People think we're selling out? Wow, that's crazy."

I nod, "Yeah, it's the latest rumor going around."

Pedro shakes his head, "We're not selling out. It's a merger. A huge opportunity for us."

I shrug. "Well, they're in the dark. They only know the office whispers."

"And what did you tell Bea?"

"I said it's like part of the company is being shared, like leasing the formal and technical IP teams."

Pedro chuckles. "You probably just fueled her curiosity."

"That was sort of the point. But she won't let it go, so I thought I'd come to you. Maybe it's time for some truth-telling?"

Pedro groans. "I wish I could say something. But Rodrigo's dragging his feet on the papers. Thought he'd be eager to sign."

I raise an eyebrow. "He's not backing out, is he?"

"No, he's still on board," Pedro reassures, his fingers drumming on the desk. "He's just swamped. Running the new office in the city solo. You know Rodrigo, Mr. Do-It-All."

"Yeah, noticed he's been MIA since Saturday."

Pedro sighs. "I can't announce anything without Dad or Rodrigo. But I'll have a word with the IP team, set up a meeting to sort things out."

"Thanks, Pedro," I say, standing up. "Now, how do I deal with Bea's inquisition?"

He grins. "You'll figure it out. You always do."

As I exit Pedro's office, Bea ambushes me. "What's the word? Spill!"

I rub my temples. "Pedro's going to talk to the IP team, but can you chill? Your hyperactive vibes are giving me a headache."

"But is he telling us today?" she presses.

"It's not a lease or a buyout. It's a merger. Happy now? Keep it on the down-low until Pedro talks to the team."

Bea squeals, clapping like a kid on Christmas morning.

"Shh! You're drawing a crowd. Keep it together, Bea," I hiss.

She looks a tad guilty. "Sorry... okay, I'm cool."

"Okay, good. Let's go get lunch at Subway and then head to the coffee shop down the street. You can have a doughnut and a soothing tea," I say, stressing the word 'soothing' for Bea's sake.

CHAPTER TWELVE

Deborah and Pedro are taking the big leap – moving in together. They look ridiculously, over-the-moon happy, and part of me is a little jealous – but it's the good kind of jealous – the kind that makes you smile and shake your head, thinking, 'Damn, they really got it together.'

It's wild to think how in just six months, Pedro and Rodrigo could become such a huge part of my life.

Pedro, now feels like a brother. I mean, how does that even happen? It's kind of crazy when you think about it, but I wouldn't have it any other way.

Then there's Rodrigo. *Oh, Rodrigo*. We're in this weird, undefined territory – definitely more than just friends. We're like a couple in everything but name. Public? Nah, we're keeping it low-key. Imagine if Deborah and Pedro knew. They'd be hounding us for double dates, and let's be real, Rodrigo and I aren't exactly the double-date types.

Rodrigo's become my best friend – the male version, obviously, because Deborah's still my girl. But with him, it's a whole other vibe. There's this niggling fear that making things public might just jinx whatever it is we have. And I'm not about to let that happen.

Deborah and Pedro were like a match struck in a dry forest – instant flames. Rodrigo and I? We're more like a slow simmer, a build-up that took a good six months to get to boiling point. The flirtation, the chemistry? It's always been there, but romance? That took its sweet time.

It's funny, you know. Sometimes I catch myself thinking, 'Are we too different?' But then he'll say something, or give me that look, and I remember why this feels so right. We're not a fairytale whirlwind like Deborah and Pedro – ours is more of a slow burn, but man, *is it burning now*.

CHAPTER THIRTEEN

RODRIGO
NOW

I'm riding this wild wave of non-stop work since Saturday. It's midweek now, and the last human interaction I had that wasn't work-related was Pedro's pity visit with pizza and beer. Spoiler: I barely grazed them. Too caught up in the chaos of setting up this new office.

My phone buzzes, speaking of the devil...

"Hey," I grunt into the phone, shuffling through a jungle of paperwork. I'm aiming for casual but probably hitting 'exhausted mess' right on the nose.

Pedro's voice is full with that brotherly concern that's as subtle as a brick. "How's it going?"

I force a chuckle, "Living the dream. You know me." My voice is about as convincing as a politician's promise.

"You sound like you're about to crash."

"Me? Never," I bluff, propping the phone between my shoulder and ear while I play Tetris with the files on my desk.

"So, Petra stopped by today," he drops casually, and just like that, he's got my full attention. The paperwork forgotten as I grab the phone.

"What about?"

"The merger," he says, and I can almost hear the smirk in his voice. "Guess what? The office is buzzing with rumors."

I straighten up. "What? How'd they even get wind of it?"

Pedro laughs. "The best part? They don't really know a thing. They think the company's being bought out."

I'm lost. "And they don't know I'm the 'big bad buyer'?"

"Bingo," he confirms. "You're the mysterious tycoon in their soap opera."

"And Petra? She clued in?"

"She's on it…"

I rub my temples. "What's the game plan?"

"We need to clear the air. Let's rope in Dad and set up a meeting. The team deserves to know they're not being sold to the highest bidder. They'll have two bosses now. Us," he suggests.

I nod to myself. "Do it. I'll be there."

—

I find myself gearing up for the big reveal to the Intellectual Property team. It's 10 a.m., and I'm finally out the door, laptop and jacket in tow. The city traffic is a beast, and I'm nostalgic for New York's chaos. A different kind of beast, but mine all the same.

I park my car, striding towards the glass doors, and there's this magnetic pull, almost instinctive, to scan the crowd for Petra.

"Get it together, Rodrigo," I scold myself, but it's like telling the tide not to turn.

I can feel the curious glances, the hushed whispers. They know I'm the catalyst for whatever news is brewing. I catch a glimpse of Petra, in her signature black – always black, like a storm cloud with the promise of thunder. I resist the urge to drink in the sight of her. She's the kind of stunning that knocks the wind out of you.

Reaching Pedro's office, the door swings open, and there's my dad with his usual quip, "Ah, there he is. Tarde como siempre!"

I brush it off, straightening my blazer. "Some of us have real work," I retort, "Not just barking orders from a throne."

Pedro jumps in. "We're all here, that's what counts. Let's get this show on the road."

We nod, a truce of sorts, and head out to face the music.

I spot Petra again, commanding the room like she owns it – which, in a way, she does. She's all poise and power, a goddess in a boardroom. I catch myself staring, but she's sharp, that one – her gaze flicks up, and our eyes lock. I flash a grin, turning away.

Pedro's voice cuts through my thoughts. "Avery!" he calls to someone downstairs, "If anyone's looking for me, I'm off the grid."

Thumbs up from Avery, and we're back in business.

"Ready for the grand finale?" Pedro asks, motioning to Dad and me.

I nod, steeling myself. It's showtime, and the leading lady is already center stage.

Striding into the meeting room, I'm acutely aware of Petra's presence behind us. She's looking like a walking fantasy in a pencil skirt black dress and killer pumps. *Focus, Rod,* your job here isn't to look at Petra's legs.

We settle in, the team flocks around the table, Petra included. Of course, she has to be in my direct line of sight. Perfect. Just the distraction I need. I steal a glance at her, and she's playing her role as Miss Efficiency, until our eyes lock. She gives me a once-over, lingering just a second too long before breaking away. *Gotcha.*

Pedro's voice cuts through the room, addressing the elephant in the room – the company's fate. "We're not being bought," he announces, setting off a visible wave of relief. "We're merging, but not totally. You get a new boss – my brother, Rodrigo," he says, throwing me a wink.

The room's eyes shift to me, and I feel the weight of their curiosity – I can't bring myself to look at Petra, *not now*.

Pedro outlines the merger specifics, separating my New York venture from this one. Then, unexpectedly, he passes the baton to me.

I stand up, feeling the stares. "Most of you don't know me—" I begin, "—I'm Rodrigo. I run a similar show in New York, specializing in Intellectual Property."

My eyes find Petra's, and she's staring, concentrated and unreadable. *What's behind those eyes, Bird?*

I break the gaze, continuing. "I wanted to focus on IP here in Seattle, and who better to work with than the best in the state?"

The room buzzes with chatter.

I raise my voice, commanding attention. "Let's hold off on questions until the end of the presentation," I suggest, offering a friendly grin. "We'll answer everything then. Deal?"

—

Post-meeting, I'm bee-lining for the kitchen when Bea, heels clicking a frantic rhythm on the granite, catches up. "Hold up," she is panting. "That smokin' hot guy from the other day is our new boss?" she asks, almost whispering, making me laugh out loud.

"God, Bea—" I say, catching my breath. "Were you even in the meeting? He's not owning us... it's a merger. We'll work with him a lot, but he doesn't own shit."

"Damn, girl," she says. "How close are you with that family? You just talked about him like you don't give a crap."

"And as a matter of fact, I don't." I clarify.

But then, a voice, smooth as silk but twice as dangerous. "Not quite sure of that, are we, Bird?"

Rodrigo. Of all the timings. My coffee can wait, but can my patience?

I pivot, Bea's going full statue mode, probably hoping invisibility comes with stillness. "Pretty sure, yeah," I say, mustering casual as I turn towards the caffeine haven.

"Need you for a sec, Bird," he says, making me turn back.

"It's Petra," I correct him, hiding my irritation behind a smile. "And I need coffee. Like, now."

Bea finally thaws, backing me up — sort of. "Seriously, she's a bear without her caffeine."

Rodrigo's grin is all mischief. "Is there ever a time when she's not a bear?"

"Post-coffee, maybe. Let's find out, shall we?" I say, heading for the kitchen.

He holds his hands up, conceding. "Not messing with the caffeine queen. Go on, your highness."

Kitchen-bound, I grab a mug, and Bea's right behind me. I pour the coffee, feeling her gaze. "What?"

"First off," Bea starts, all dreamy-eyed, "if he ever called me something adorable like that, I'd be dead."

I lean back against the fridge, "Adorable? Please. That's his shorthand for 'Petra, the walking disaster.'"

She's relentless. "Second, if he wanted a chat with me, I'd drop everything. No questions asked."

"Priorities, Bea. Coffee first," I say, taking a protective sip. "Non-negotiable."

Her eyes light up. "Third, seriously, how long have you two known each other? There's some serious sparkage there."

I cut her off, stepping away from the fridge, coffee in tow. "No sparks, zero chemistry, end of story." I head out, coffee cup raised like a shield. "Gotta go see the new boss. Fingers crossed, with caffeine on my side, no crimes will be committed today."

—

RODRIGO

"So, big shot New York lawyer ditches running but can't kick the smokes, huh?" Pedro says with a sneaky smile.

I exhale a smoke ring, "Running's on pause, not quit. Planning to hit the pavement again after your birthday dinner. Hopefully, by then, life's a tad less crazy." I sigh, gazing into the distance. Running used to be my jam, my escape from the world. But ever since I've been back, it's all work, stress, and these damn cigarettes.

Pedro glances skyward. "Yeah, hope so."

I tease him, "Aren't you supposed to be upstairs with Mr. Gomez?"

He shrugs off the mention of our father. "Dad's on a call. Seized the moment for a break."

"Our little chat went well, huh?"

Pedro nods. "Smooth as silk. But now, we've gotta loop in Petra. Dad wants her to be the first to sign the new contract."

I scoff, smoke curling from my lips. "Is he afraid she will leave your company to work for me in New York? Is he that confident in his management skills?"

"Nah," Pedro returns my gaze. "It's more about setting a tone. If Petra signs, everyone else will follow suit."

I chuckle, flicking ash. "Let's hope that contract caps her coffee intake, or we're bankrupt in a week." I pause, a thought striking me. "Hey, we gotta sign our part first, remember?"

"Fuck," Pedro curses, bolting inside. I hear him apologize for crashing into someone.

I glance around and there's Petra, coffee in hand, looking like a force of nature.

"What do you need from me?" she asks, arms crossed, an eyebrow arched.

"Don't flatter yourself, Bird, it's not just me. Pedro and the big boss want a word too." I drop my cigarette and stroll past her, feeling her gaze burn my back.

As I head inside, Petra's following, her heels clicking a rhythmic protest on the granite. She pauses to ditch her coffee at a desk, then hisses at me, "Could you be any more obnoxious?"

I lead the way, ignoring her comment. "No idea what you're talking about."

Petra's keeping pace with me, her voice low. "You just show up, all 'let's talk,' and then it's not even you who needs to chat. It's like you're fishing for excuses to hang with me."

Her comment makes me grin. "Maybe I do enjoy your company," I murmur, leaning in just enough to watch a hint of pink blossom on her cheeks. She doesn't shy away, and that's my Petra — always holding her ground.

But then she stumbles, a misstep on the stairs. Quick as a flash, I'm there, my hand at her waist, the other steadying her arm. *She's close, too close*, her breath hitching, eyes squeezing shut. A few onlookers pause, but I'm too caught up in the moment to care.

"Still think you're not clumsy?" I tease, holding her gaze. There's a flicker of something — annoyance, embarrassment — before she steps back, putting space between us.

"Just testing your reflexes," she says, trying to sound casual.

"Testing?" I arch an eyebrow, my smirk in place. "Well, consider me your reliable guinea pig. But how about a heads-up next time?"

As she ascends the stairs, Petra pauses, rotating her ankle. That tattoo catches my eye — a vine with delicate flowers, wrapping around her ankle. It's always intrigued me, the way it seems to capture her essence — strong yet graceful.

"You okay?" I ask as we reach the top.

She winces slightly, biting her lip. "Might've sprained it," she admits, her stubborn streak showing.

I glance at her ankle. "Ice might help."

She gives me a dry look. "I've got it under control, but thanks for playing doctor." With that, she turns, her stride confident as she heads for the conference room.

CHAPTER FOURTEEN

PETRA

My stomach is having its own rebellious concert, loudly protesting the lack of food since breakfast. I glance at Rodrigo and his father, who are deeply engrossed in their contract-signing ritual. Every word, every initial, examined with the intensity of a detective. I've already breezed through my contract, so when they finally finish, I sign mine with a dramatic flair that could rival any calligrapher. *The deal is sealed.*

My ankle, however, is a different story – a painful, throbbing narrative. These heels, more torture devices than shoes, are definitely not helping. When I finally manage to stand, it's like walking on a bed of nails. I hobble out, trying to maintain a semblance of grace, but by the time I reach the bathroom, my composure shatters. I lean against the wall, cursing every deity known to man, tears threatening to spill.

And then, there's Rodrigo, his hand suddenly wrapping around my waist with the unexpectedness of a plot twist. Great, just the audience I need for my meltdown.

"Are you okay?"

"I'm good," I reply, trying to mask the pain.

"I'm not buying the brave act, Bird."

"It's just a sprain," I say, gritting my teeth as a wave of pain hits.

Rodrigo doesn't buy my act for a second and examines my ankle, now swollen like a storm cloud. "We need to ice this, pronto," his tone brooking no argument, guiding me back to the meeting room. He disappears for a moment, returning like a knight with his shield – only his shield is a bag of ice wrapped in a towel.

Kneeling down, he places the ice with a gentleness that's disarming, sending some shivers up my spine that have nothing to do with the cold. "This should help," he murmurs, his dark green eyes meeting mine.

"Thanks," I manage, attempting to sound cool, but failing miserably. He's still kneeling there, his gaze shifting from my ankle to my face.

"Your makeup's a bit messed up," he observes.

Crap. I quickly cover my eyes, mortified. But he just chuckles, standing up and slipping his hands in his pockets like he's got all the time in the world.

There's something about Rodrigo being this caring that throws me off balance. My heart's a traitor, fluttering like a crazy thing – and I'm just here, trying not to fall for it.

"It's not the eyeliner, don't worry. That one is perfect. It's the beige stuff and a bit of the eyelashes stuff," Rodrigo says, pointing at my face with an amusing lack of makeup vocabulary.

I chuckle, "You mean my concealer and mascara. It's almost adorable how you pretend to know about makeup."

Pedro swings the door open, his eyes widening at the sight. "Everything okay here? Petty, what happened?"

"Just a little tumble down the stairs. Sprained my ankle."

"You should see a doctor," Pedro suggests, concern etched in his features.

Rodrigo saunters over, his gaze locking with mine. "Definitely doctor material. Can't argue with two bosses, can you, Bird?"

"I'm fine, really. Just need some ice and painkillers. I have work to do, can't go to a doctor now."

Rodrigo leans down, his hands gently pushing me back into the chair. "When your bosses give you an order, what do you do?" His voice is teasing, but concern is definitely there.

I groan, "Okay, but I don't want to go to the doctor. Some painkillers will do. It's just a sprain."

"Painkillers won't do a thing if you don't rest. You have to go home and rest, elevate your foot, and put a lot of ice on your ankle," Rodrigo's tone firm.

"Are you a doctor now?" I mock, trying to hide my growing smile.

"Let's just say I'm more in tune with common sense than someone who tumbles downstairs," he shoots back with a smirk.

Pedro steps in, "Enough, you two. Petra, you're off until Monday. No arguments."

I'm flustered. "But my work, Pedro! I have deadlines!"

"We'll manage. Bea can cover the international stuff," Pedro reassures.

"But I'm not ready to just...leave," I protest.

Rodrigo interjects, "I'll get you a laptop. Everything will be set up. You won't miss a beat."

His unexpected kindness catches me off guard.

"Is that okay?" he asks, his eyes holding mine.

"Yeah, fine," I mumble, looking away to hide my blush.

"Good. Now, go home," Pedro orders gently.

"I can't drive like this," I admit, glancing out of the window.

"I'll take you," Rodrigo volunteers quickly.

"And my car?" I ask.

"Don't worry about it. We'll sort it out. Right now, you getting better is the priority."

I simply nod. It's hard to argue when Rodrigo's looking at me like that, like I'm the only thing that matters, even though I know that's not the truth.

"I'll come back for it when I drop you off at home and come back here to get your stuff so you can work from home," Rodrigo tries to solve my problem. "That is if you let me drive your car, of course." He adds with a grin.

"I don't have many options, do I?" I shoot him a doubtful look. "Just don't mess with my radio settings. And if you adjust my seat, you're dead."

"Noted, Bird," he winks. "But I make no promises about not testing its speed limits."

Pedro leans in, planting a brotherly kiss on my forehead. "Rodrigo, take care of her, will you? She's as stubborn as they come."

I snark back, "I'm right here, you know. I can handle myself."

Pedro throws a knowing glance over his shoulder. "Of course, you can." He exits, throwing over his shoulder, "And make sure she eats. She's a notorious meal-skipper."

Rodrigo arches an eyebrow at me. "Looks like I'm your nanny now. What tales have you been spinning?" he asks extending his hand.

"I don't need your help," I say, but the truth is, standing up is looking like a Herculean task right now.

"Fine. Prepare to be carried out, Cinderella-style," he threatens with a glint in his eye that says he's not entirely joking.

"Go ahead, I dare you. But brace yourself for a kick or two. I'm no damsel in distress."

"Tempting, but let's not cause a scene."

I reluctantly accept his hand, and he steadies me.

"Heels are a no-go, Bird. Wouldn't want you taking another flight down the stairs."

"Ugh, stop being so reasonable, for fuck's sake." I grumble, slipping off the murderous shoes again.

"Come on, give them to me," he says, holding out his other hand, waiting for me to give him the shoes.

"No! I am very capable of carrying my own shoes, thank you." I spit, and as I fumble with the ice pack and my shoes, true to my 'clumsy bird' title, I drop everything. "Oh, come on..." I mutter.

Rodrigo chuckles, squatting down to gather my scattered belongings. "Let the expert handle this. No more protests."

We finally make it downstairs, and luckily, there's hardly anyone in the office to see me looking like a disaster – it's lunchtime, and my humiliation is spared.

Outside, he ushers me into his sleek BMW. "Buckle up. I'm an excellent driver, I promise."

As we drive, I realize we're not heading towards Pedro and Deborah's. "Where are we going? This isn't the way."

He grins, eyes on the road. "A little detour. Thought I'd surprise you. You know, cheer up the injured bird."

"I don't like surprises."

He looks at me with that infuriatingly charming smile. "Trust me, you'll love this one."

—

As Rodrigo glides his car into the garage, he clicks a button, and the door majestically opens. He kills the engine, turning to me with that trademark grin. "Welcome to Casa del Rodrigo!"

I have to admit, it's a pretty impressive house. It's a two-story house with at least four bedrooms, and it looks like it's been recently renovated. The exterior is painted a crisp white, and the yard is impeccably maintained.

"Just wait here, Bird. Just need to grab something quickly." With that, he dashes into the house. Minutes later, I hear panting. Before I can process, a golden furball leaps into view.

"Saskya!" I exclaim, as the golden retriever plants slobbery kisses all over my face. "Hey, pretty girl," I coo, scratching behind her ears. She's a bundle of joy, and I'm instantly smitten.

Rodrigo saunters back, looking smug. "See? I'm good with surprises."

"You got lucky this time," I say.

He tosses a bottle of painkillers onto my lap. "And these are for later. Just in case."

After a short drive, we finally get to the apartment building, and Rodrigo smoothly parks the car in front of the main entrance. As he hops out, Saskya's tail goes into overdrive, excitement everywhere. He opens my door, and a realization hits me like a ton of bricks. "Crap, I don't have my keys."

"Good thing I'm always one step ahead of you, Bird." He fishes out a pair of keys from his pocket. "Extra keys, just in case."

"Show-off," I mumble.

He helps me out of the car, my bare feet hitting the cool street. "I got your shoes," he says, juggling my heels in one hand.

"And I've got the painkillers," I say, clutching the bottle and the ice pack.

Saskya bounds out of the backseat, as Rodrigo supports me as we head to my building, the door held open by his free hand.

Hobbling into the elevator, I shoot Rodrigo a glare. "You know I'm a stairs person," I grumble, but he just hits the button with a smirk.

Saskya's not a fan either, her tail tucked between her legs. "Hey, it's just a fancy moving room," Rodrigo coaxes, scratching her ears and she relaxes a bit. He looks at me and smiles, and I feel a warmth in my chest.

We finally get into the apartment, and Rodrigo helps me to the couch, putting my shoes down next to me. He takes the melting ice and wet towel from my hands and, without a word, puts them in the sink and heads over to the freezer. He then retrieves another bag of ice and, after opening a drawer in the kitchen cabinets, takes out another towel.

"Here, Ice Queen," he hands me a fresh pack. "Ten on, ten off. Got it?"

"Wow, Doctor Rodrigo. Where'd you get your degree? WebMD University?"

"Funny, Bird. But some of us know how to use Google for more than stalking exes."

I open my mouth to retort, but my ankle throbs a silent protest. Truce, for now.

"Also," he adds, "Don't take the painkillers just yet. You haven't eaten anything, and they might upset your stomach." He turns his back and heads towards the door.

He's halfway to the door when I call out, "Hey, where are you going?"

He turns, a teasing glint in his eyes. "Scared you'll miss my charming company?"

"Hardly," I shoot back. "Just don't want to be stranded without painkillers and... company."

He chuckles. "Relax, Bird. I'm on a food and purse rescue mission. Your beloved sushi is on the menu."

"Sushi?" My ears perk up, and he knows it. He's always known my weak spots.

"And your car will be in good hands. Promise not to change your radio presets," he adds with a wink, heading out.

I sink back, Saskya snuggling beside me. "We're in for an interesting day, huh, girl?"

The door clicks shut, and I'm alone, with a melting ice pack, and a dog who's probably judging my life choices. But sushi's on the way, and Rodrigo's surprising me in more ways than one. Maybe, just maybe, this day won't be so bad after all.

CHAPTER FIFTEEN

RODRIGO

Striding out of the apartment, phone pressed to my ear, I hit Ava's number. She's my right hand, my go-to, the only one who gets my chaos. We're a New York duo turned Seattle team – she's my assistant, sure, but also the closest thing I have to a best friend. I trust about as many people as I have fingers on one hand, and Ava's right there at the top of that short list. That's why I lugged her across the country with me. No strings attached in her life – no present boyfriend, no kids, no pets.

"Ava," I say, "I need you to cancel all of the meetings I have this afternoon and reschedule them, please."

"But Rod, you have an important client today, remember?" she shoots back. She's not wrong. I've been chasing this client like a cat after a laser pointer. But priorities have shifted – today, it's all about a certain dog-loving, ankle-spraining enigma.

"Yeah, I know," I reply, slipping into my car. "But something's come up. It's... urgent."

Ava's silence tells me she's not buying the vague excuse. "When do you want to reschedule?"

I'm scrambling for dates in my head. "Check my calendar. Make it work." Ava's good at that – making the impossible happen.

"Got it. Anything else?"

"Just keep the ship afloat, Ava. I'm off-radar for the rest of the day."

Ending the call, I head back to my dad's office. There's a buzz of activity, but I zero in on the girl who'd been chatting with Petra earlier. She's a splash of color in the monochrome world of office life.

"Hey," I start, and she's all blushes and batted eyelashes. "Need a favor. Can you round up Petra's stuff? She's out with an injury."

Bea's concern is instant. "Is she okay?"

"Just a twisted ankle. But she left her stuff here." I flash a smile. "Can you help?"

"Of course," she replies, already on the move.

As she scurries off, I call after her, "Sorry, I didn't catch your name."

"Bea," she answers, a shy grin on her face.

"Thanks, Bea. You're a lifesaver."

With that, I pivot, heading for my brother's office.

Zipping past my brother's glass-walled office, I spot him tangled in a meeting. Perfect timing for a quick call. "Yo, Liam," I say, my voice casual. "Got a sec for a favor?" Liam's my go-to tech wizard, the kind of guy who can hack the Pentagon but uses his powers to watch cat videos in 4K.

"Hit me," he says, ever ready.

"Need a tech miracle, buddy. Can you morph everything from a desktop to a laptop? Like, today?" I ask, cutting straight to the chase.

"Piece of cake," Liam responds. "I'll swing by. When?"

"How's an hour sound?" I suggest, already planning the next move in my head.

"Done deal," he agrees.

My stomach is screaming for food as Saskya, the fluffiest couch companion, snoozes on my lap. We're binging 'Say Yes to the Dress', anything to distract me from the throb in my ankle.

The door swings open and Rodrigo strides in, breaking our trance. Saskya's tail goes into overdrive as he drapes my coat and slings my purse over his shoulder like it's the latest men's fashion. He dumps a feast of takeout on the kitchen island before sauntering over.

"Did you miss my charming presence, Bird?" he teases.

"I never pegged Rodrigo Gomez as a shoulder bag guy," I shoot back, "But hey, it does wonders for your eyes."

He chuckles, a sarcastic sound that's music to my ears. "Hilarious," he deadpans, unloading food. "Oh, and Bea sends her love. She's the one who played your personal shopper today."

Attempting to stand, a jolt of pain chains me back down. "I'll call her up post-food," I wince. "I'm starving here."

"Who said you could leave the couch?" he challenges, with that bossy tone I hate... *not.*

"Since when did you become the boss of me?"

"Technically, since this morning," he smirks. "Work humor."

"Touché," I concede. "But hunger trumps hierarchy. I'm not a couch potato by choice." I attempt a pout, earning a smile from him.

"Trust me, the couch is where you belong right now," he insists, that all-knowing look in his eyes that drives me nuts.

"I'm not a toddler, Rodrigo. I want to sit at the island," I demand, arms crossed. Independence is my middle name, even if it leads to questionable choices.

He eyes me like a puzzle he's figuring out. "You're a handful, aren't you?" he says, his touch light but firm on my arm. I shrug it off, stubbornly standing up, limping toward the kitchen.

"I'm fine on my own," I insist, "And I'm not a handful. I just don't fancy being a couch ornament all day."

"Sure," he mumbles, eyes trailing me. "Just try not to take another dive, okay, Bird?"

"I'm a pro," I call back, reaching the island with a triumphant turn. "See? Still upright. Your nurse duties can relax."

Rodrigo's unpacking sushi like he's diffusing a bomb, all focus and no fun. "Just don't go breaking anything else, Bird," he says, eyeing me. "I'm not worried about you, but I can't have Pedro and Deborah grilling me for your double dose of disaster."

"Charming, as always," I shoot back, trying to shrug off the sting. Then I spot the gunkans, and it's like Christmas came early. "Gunkans!" I cheer, throwing my hands up, startling Saskya. "Whoa, sorry, baby," I whisper, patting her. Rodrigo hands me chopsticks with zero fanfare. His face is a blank canvas. "Thanks," I mutter, grabbing them.

"Don't get too excited and stab yourself," he teases, the corners of his mouth finally betraying a grin. The man's got two modes – Mr. Serious and Mr. Smirk. It's a dizzying switch.

"Funny guy," I say, pointing a chopstick at him.

"You're welcome," he says, pretending it's a compliment. "Humor's one of my many gifts."

"What else you got? Knife juggling? Lion taming? Cracking quantum physics equations?"

That gets me a cocky eyebrow raise and a dangerously close lean-in. "Curious about my hidden talents, Bird?" His voice is a low rumble, his breath warm on my skin.

I turn away, cheeks flaming. Not giving him the pleasure of seeing me flustered, I focus on the sushi. "I'll pass on your 'talents'. They're probably as overrated as you."

"Ouch," he feigns hurt. "You're missing out. My skills are legendary."

I lean in, "Oh, do tell."

His grin is all trouble. "Only one way to find out."

I play along, my heart doing a weird little dance. "Not sure if I can handle the Rodrigo experience."

His laugh is a sound that does things to me. "I'll be gentle, promise."

Right then, his phone goes off. 'Ava' flashes on the screen. He swallows his sushi and grabs the call. "Hey, babe, what's up?"

Babe? My mind hits a brick wall. *Who is Ava? And why is she 'babe'?*

I watch him nod and grunt through the call, finally saying, "Can't today. You're amazing. Tomorrow, I'll make it up to you."

I'm hit with a wave of nausea so strong it could knock over a heavyweight. Rodrigo and someone else? My mind's spinning faster than a top.

Get it together, Petra. This is not the time for a meltdown.

Snapping back to reality, I find Rodrigo's back in a serious relationship with his sushi, his phone abandoned like yesterday's news. "Are you okay? You look like you just walked in on a ghost," he asks, not missing a beat.

I glare at him, trying to look unbothered. "Yeah, I'm fine," I snap, and to prove my point, I stuff another sushi roll into my mouth like it's a gold medal event.

But the question gnaws at me like a hungry rat: *Who in the world is Ava?*

—

RODRIGO

My phone lights up with Ava's name, and I'm half-listening, half-watching Petra annihilate those gunkans like it's her personal mission. She's always been a sucker for them, and some things just don't change, do they?

"Hey, babe, what's up?" I say, casually flicking off a stray rice grain.

"That big shot client you bailed on? He's here, throwing a hissy fit. Says you promised him the moon and stars."

I sigh, glancing over at Petra, who's now eyeing her sushi like it owes her money. "Ava, I'm really tied up here."

"I know you can't, but I had to buy some time here, and I told him I would try to talk to you anyway. I will tell him you had a family emergency and guarantee that you'll talk to him tomorrow, if not in person, then at least on the phone. Is that okay?"

"Yes, thank you. You're a lifesaver."

"Ha, 'lifesaver.' Keep that in mind," she quips, her laugh tinkling through the line.

"I promise I'll make it up to you tomorrow."

"Think an extra vacay day might just cover it," she bargains.

I laugh, already picturing her on a beach somewhere. "You got it. Thank you once again. See you tomorrow."

"Yeah, and you are lucky I've got your back. Remember, you owe me," she singsongs, and then we're done.

Phone down, I catch Petra giving her sushi the stink eye. "Are you okay? You look like you just walked in on a ghost."

Her comeback's cooler than ice. "Yeah, I'm fine." She's stuffing her face with sushi again, but something's off.

I grab the painkillers from earlier and slide them over. "Might want to pop one of those."

She swallows a mouthful of sushi, downs a pill, and shoots me a look that could start fires. "Thanks, boss."

"How's the ankle?"

"Oh, fantastic. Planning to run a marathon. I frankly just didn't want to work, so I played the sprain card."

"Faking an injury to dodge work? You're full of surprises."

"Where's my laptop?" she demands, suddenly all business.

"It's being sorted. You'll have it by tomorrow."

"But I need it now, Rodrigo." She's practically whining.

"Nope, you're on lockdown. Shower, then back to couch arrest. Doctor's orders."

"Ever been told you're a control freak?"

"Only by people who can't handle their own lives," I shoot back.

She stands, all drama. "Fine. I'm off to my cell, then. Thanks, Warden Rodrigo."

I mock-salute. "At your service, always." All I can do is smile as she hobbles away.

—

I'm marooned on the couch in a sea of slumber – Saskya's in dreamland on one side, and Petra, in her fuzzy pajamas, has zonked out mid-sit on the other. Me? I'm wide awake, enduring what seems like a never-ending marathon of wedding disasters on TV. Because that's my idea of a good time...

Just as I'm about to lose it to boredom, my phone saves the day. It's Pedro, "Heading out now. Will ping you when I'm there so we can go get your car." As I'm thumbing back a reply, another message slides in, "P.S. Got the laptop."

I sneak a glance at Petra, all innocent in her sleep. She's like a kitten now, not the usual spitfire. I'm contemplating waking her when she mumbles something sassy in her sleep. Even unconscious, she's got a bite.

Now Saskya's stirring and Petra's using me as her personal pillow. *I'm trapped.* I give Petra a gentle nudge. "Hey, Bird, time to wake up." She just grunts, and I'm struck with a genius idea. "Sask, show Petra some love, will ya?"

Saskya, ever the obedient pup, leans in and plants a wet one on Petra's cheek. Petra jolts awake, shoving Saskya off, and I'm cracking up at the chaos I've sparked.

Petra squints at me, trying to piece together the situation. "What the—"

I lay it out for her. "Options were limited, Bird. Either Saskya here gives you a wake-up call, or I do. But let's face it, you haven't earned the privilege of my premium wake-up service. So, I figured the doggy method was more your speed."

She looks at me like I've grown two heads. "And what's the rate for this premium service?"

"Well, it's a dynamic pricing model," I explain, "A peck's cheap, but if you're aiming for that movie-style, rain-soaked kiss, that'll cost you a small fortune in loyalty points."

Petra looks like I've just offered her a week-old sandwich. "I'll stick with the dog, thanks. Your 'services' aren't exactly in high demand."

"Your loss," I shoot back. "I'm a legend in the kiss department, you know."

She brushes off my pitch, taking a swig of water.

"So, Pedro's about to show up. Time for me to bounce," I say, shifting gears.

The room goes silent, and Petra looks a bit down. "You think my ankle will hold up for Pedro's dinner on Saturday?"

I pretend to ponder, "Considering how much you've been abusing it, I'd say it's probably gonna fall off by morning." Her face drains of color, and I can't hold back a laugh. "I'm just messing with you. Take it easy, and you'll be fine for Saturday. Just maybe skip the high heels."

"What, scared I'll out-height you in my stilettos?"

"Please, Bird, you're what, 4'9"? You're hobbit-sized compared to me!"

Her jaw hits the floor. "First of all, I am a towering 5'2", so watch it. Even hobbits would crane their necks looking up to me, thank you very much."

"Oh, absolutely, a real giant among... toddlers." I crack a laugh.

Petra's not backing down, her arms folded in a stance of mock indignation. "And FYI, I'll be killing it in those heels, new boots. And it's not like you know much about ankles, Dr. Google."

I flash her a teasing grin. "Let's just say I've picked up a few tips from Mom's medical rants. I might not have a degree, but I've got some solid ankle intel." Just then, my phone jingles with Pedro's ringtone, "As much as I enjoy our height debates and your future in footwear, I've got to take this. Duty calls, Bird."

CHAPTER SIXTEEN

PETRA

Okay, I've got to admit — though only in the privacy of my own head where Rodrigo's nagging can't reach — the whole ice-and-meds routine is actually doing wonders for my ankle even though it's not perfect, which reminds me that tonight is Pedro's birthday dinner, and here I am, eyeing those killer lace-up boots I bought with Deborah.

Damn it, why do I let Rodrigo get in my head? He's like a walking, talking conscience with a bad haircut — he's the Jiminy Cricket of my life.

"Hey," Deborah breezes into my room, her tone all casual concern. "How's the ankle today?"

I give her a thumbs-up, putting on my best 'all good' face. "So much better, you wouldn't believe!"

She steps in, eyeing my laptop that's basically become a permanent extension of my lap. "You're not working, are you?" There's that tone, teetering on the edge of full-on big sister scolding.

"Just... online window shopping," I lie with a casual tap on the keyboard.

She lets out a sigh that's all 'I'm not buying it'. "Petra, seriously? It's the weekend. Close the laptop, embrace life!"

I play the innocent card. "Just tying up some loose ends—"

She cuts me off, throwing her hands up like she's about to start a sermon. "It's barely morning and you're already buried in work? Do you ever take a break?"

"Fine, fine, I'm shutting it down!" I snap the laptop shut, surrendering.

Deborah nods in victory, "That's more like it."

I hop off the bed, rummaging through my drawer. "What's the game plan for tonight?"

"Dinner at 7."

I half-listen, still digging through my stuff. "And the guest list?"

She pauses, probably doing mental math. "Around forty, I think... or more, maybe?"

"Got it, a whole crowd," I mutter, finally finding what I need.

"And since you're practically family now, you're at the VIP table. That means Pedro's parents, his sister, me, and... oh, Rodrigo," Deborah announces with a naughty smirk.

"A cozy family dinner with Rodrigo? Great, I'll have to mind my p's and q's and avoid spilling wine on Pedro's mom."

"They're all lovely," she says, following me to the bathroom.

I stop and turn to her. "Dee, I'm breaking bread with Rodrigo – that's like juggling grenades. Plus, I will have the big boss breathing down my neck. What could possibly go wrong?"

Her eyes light up. "You'll love Sofia, though – Pedro and Rodrigo's little sister. She's only twenty but has more spark than a fireworks show. She keeps Rodrigo in check, so there's your partner in crime."

"An ally in the trenches," I chuckle. "And to be fair, it's not me stirring the pot all the time, it's mostly Rodrigo."

Deborah's got that look, "You know what I think?"

I twist the shower handle like I'm launching a rocket. "Nope, and I'm pretty sure I don't want to."

Deborah's grin widens, like she's just cracked the Da Vinci Code. "I think all that bickering? It's just foreplay. It's like you guys have this trade secret for that messy relationship of yours. Love and hate, all mixed up together. I think the more you guys fight, the more you fall for each other."

I practically choke on the steam. "Fall for Rodrigo? Dee, have you gone off the deep end?"

What does this woman know? I am not asking... better not to know.

"For real, it's like you two are in a rom-com, stuck on repeat. It's bizarrely cute, in a 'yell at the TV' kind of way."

I'm half-laughing, half-groaning. "Rodrigo and I? We're just brewing a storm, trust me. It's like mixing oil and water – a spectacle, but no heart."

She wags a finger, "Ah, but you know, even storms have a bit of electricity. Once upon a time, you guys were like two peas in a pod," she starts, but I'm quick to slam that door shut.

"Key word: 'were'. That was before...well, before everything happened," I dismiss the idea with a flick of my hand. "Old friendships don't equate to some hidden, smoldering romance. That's Hollywood, not real life. That's just... absurd."

Deborah chuckles, poking the bear. "Did I touch a raw nerve there?"

I cast a longing look at the shower, seeing my escape. "Can I just get a shower without your Cupid arrows flying around?"

She backs away, hands up, playing the innocent. "Okay, okay, I'll back off. But think about it, will you?"

The door clicks shut behind her, and I shout after her, "Not in this lifetime!" But she's already out of earshot, probably smirking in victory.

—

RODRIGO

Leaning back in my chair, I bask in the sun outside the restaurant. Sofia's lost in her phone, probably texting her latest crush, when Mom hits me with the million-dollar question, "How's the Seattle office going?"

"Going well," I reply, trying to keep it cool. "You chat with Pedro about it?" I'm fishing for info.

"About the office?"

"Yeah," I try my best to keep my face unreadable.

She shakes her head, "Haven't seen your brother in some time, actually."

I lean in, ready to drop the bomb. "I made a deal with Dad…"

Her eyes do this little dance, like she's surprised but won't show it. "And what kind of deal are we talking about?"

I lock eyes with her. "Pedro and I… we had this idea of merging the companies. Dad's on board."

Sofia's head snaps up, her eyebrows climbing to her hairline. "You what? You and Dad, in the same boat?"

"Weren't you like sending nudes to your boyfriend or something?" I nod towards her phone with a smirk.

Sofia scowls. "Gross, Rodrigo."

Mom shoots me that 'behave yourself' glare, but there's a twinkle in her eye. "Rodrigo..."

"Yeah, Dad and I shook on it. It's good for the business, keeps me and Pedro in the loop," I explain, stretching back.

Mom's smile turns genuine, "That's wonderful, cariño!" She might be New York through and through, but she can pull off Spanish like a native. That's the New York love story – the city where it all started for me. "But now your father has a stake in your company?" Mom's got that concerned look.

"No, no," I assure her. "It's just about pooling resources and clients. It's a delicate balance. And don't worry, he's not touching my New York company. That's my baby."

Out of the corner of my eye, I catch Sofia's head bobbing like she's watching tennis, totally engrossed in the family drama.

Mom breaks into a warm smile. "I'm just happy you boys are getting along. It's good news."

As the waiter brings our food, Mom takes the chance to change gears.

"So, about Pedro's birthday dinner," she starts, spearing some kale, "Got a date?"

I shrug, tackling my lasagna. "Flying solo."

"Not one woman at your office caught your eye?"

"Exactly," I say, hoping to shut down that line of inquiry.

Mom looks skeptical, but Sofia jumps in, "C'mon, Mom, no one's brave enough to take on Rodrigo full-time."

"I'm not your mirror, Sis." I say, making her sneak in a kick under the table that makes me wince.

Mom's giving us that warning look, "Kids, please," she says, as she goes back to her salmon.

"So, how do you feel about Dad being there tonight?" I ask casually, sipping my water.

Mom shrugs it off, "It's Pedro's night. We're there to celebrate, that's it."

"But it's still a thing, right?" I probe. "You two, same room, it's not exactly a casual Tuesday."

Mom offers a soft smile. "I'll manage. What, there will be like sixty people?"

Sofia can't resist joining the fun. "Yeah, sixty people, probably half of them women, and none of them willing to put up with Rodrigo."

I grin, seizing the moment, "Mom, be honest, after Pedro and me, why'd you go for round three? Sofia came out with a 'return to sender' note – she's broken."

She swats at my hand, feigning absolute horror. "I'm not the broken one, you are!"

"Let's not forget Exhibit A: The great nude text scandal at lunchtime." I tease.

Mom is caught between amusement and exasperation. "Do you two ever take a break?"

Sofia's indignant, putting on a show of mock outrage. "For the millionth time, I am not sending nudes!"

I dramatically shield my eyes, playing along. "My innocence is at stake here! Keep that scandalous phone at bay!"

With that, she clicks her phone shut, her laughter ringing out.

—

"Ready to go?" Deborah sweeps into the room, fastening her earrings, her gaze landing on Pedro and me, prepped and primed for the night.

"Just zipping up," I quip, struggling with the stubborn zipper on my boots.

Deborah throws me a knowing look. "High heels, really? Quite the daredevil move with your 'Ankle-gate'."

I toss my hair back, "Fear not, I'm practically a walking miracle."

But Pedro's not buying it, "You sure you shouldn't be babying that ankle instead of playing runway model?"

I sigh theatrically, stand, and give them my best runway twirl. "Behold, as good as new!"

Deborah remains skeptical, eyeing my heels like they're little traitors. "Fine, but swear to me, at the slightest hint of an 'ouch', those skyscrapers are coming off. Flats or bust!"

"Scout's honor," I salute her, half-serious, half-joking.

Pedro's all smiles, extending his arm like a true-blue escort. "Let's turn my birthday into legend."

Deborah's not finished, though. "Wait a sec, you planning to magic up flats out of thin air if those heels betray you?"

I flash her a grin. "I'll just brave the pain like a hero."

Deborah's all big sister mode. "No way, missy. Back to your room, fetch those backup flats."

I chuckle, making a beeline for my room, grabbing my reliable black Dr. Martens – always good for a Plan B.

Returning with boots in tow, I flash a 'ready to roll' nod. It's time to hit the town – if my ankle decides to play diva, I'm prepped for a quick-change act.

—

Pedro's Audi RS6 purrs to a stop, and we can already spot the crowd milling about inside the restaurant, our own private hive for the night.

We slip out of the car, and a girl appears, gliding towards us in shimmery silver sandals, a vision in red that clings to her like it's part of her. Light brown locks trail her like a comet's tail – has to be Sofia, even if her porcelain doll complexion and delicate look stand out against the darker, classic features of her brothers. Those green eyes of hers? They're catching glances left and right, a couple of shades brighter and definitely more mischief than the boys. She launches at Pedro with a bear hug. "Happy Birthday!" she exclaims, her embrace warmer than a summer day.

Pedro's laughter rings true as he hugs her back. "Thanks, Sof."

And here comes Rodrigo, "Feliz Cumpleaños, bro," followed by a woman who's like Sofia but dialed up in elegance. She envelopes Pedro in a hug that screams 'mom love'.

"Happy Birthday, sweetheart," she coos, a kiss on his cheek sealing the deal.

Rodrigo's eyes land on my heels. "Surviving in those ankle breakers?" he teases, a smirk playing on his lips.

I wave off his comment, my eyes on Deborah meeting the family. "I've got a backup plan. Deborah's got flats in the car, just in case."

His smirk widens. "Thoughtful. Wouldn't want you turning the birthday dinner into your personal pity party with ankle woes."

I lean closer, my voice low but firm. "You know what's really gonna kill the vibe? Your endless chattering. Maybe zip it and let Pedro enjoy his day?"

He raises an eyebrow, clearly entertained. "Was gonna offer you a drink, but now I'm rethinking."

"No thanks. I've got a strict policy on drinking company, and you're not on the list."

Rodrigo's mom beams at me, "And who might this lovely lady be?"

Rodrigo gives a half-hearted intro, "This is Petra, Mom."

I step in with a bright smile, "Nice to meet you, ma'am. I'm Petra."

Evelyn's hug is unexpectedly warm. "Call me Evelyn," she insists. Rodrigo's watching, an unreadable look flickering in his eyes, but he's back to poker-face mode when she turns to him. "And how are you related to my devilish son?"

Rodrigo's lips tighten. "We're not really related."

That's when I jump in. "Oh, I'm Deborah's friend. Known Pedro and her forever. I'm like the honorary member – the quirky one."

Evelyn chuckles, a sound like music. Even Rodrigo's lips twitch. "Quirky, indeed."

"Not quirky," Rodrigo corrects. "More like a bird."

Evelyn's eyes sparkle. "Birds always find a way to make any place home."

Sofia breezes in, her energy infectious. "Hey!" she greets me before whisking Evelyn away. "Mom, let's grab our seats."

As the family disperses, I'm left navigating the crowd in my heels, feeling like I'm marching to my own doom.

Finally reaching the table, I'm contemplating my footwear choices when Rodrigo slides into the seat opposite me. The room's still abuzz with chatter, leaving us in our own little world. Rodrigo leans in, "Avoiding drinks but stuck with me for dinner. Can't seem to keep away, can you, Bird?"

My smile is strained as I reply, "Believe me, if I knew I'd be dining with your ego, I would've opted for a cozy night with ramen and reality TV."

Our bickering is suddenly side-tracked by Sofia, who swoops in with a furrowed brow, looking like she's about to unravel a mystery. "Seen Dad yet?" she asks Rodrigo.

Rodrigo looks up from our eye-war, throwing her a look of mock surprise. "What? Am I on Dad-duty now?" he shoots back. He deftly sidesteps her attempt at a playful slap, his grin all mischievous charm.

Sofia presses on, her eyes flitting to her phone. "He's supposed to show up, right?" There's a hint of worry as she scrolls through her messages.

Rodrigo suggests, "Why not give him a ring?" Then, with a sly grin, he adds, "Or is your phone just for more... scandalous chats?"

Sofia's eyes snap up, "SHUT..." before cutting herself off. She shoots me a quick, complicit smile my way, diffusing the tension. Rodrigo's chuckle follows her as she turns, dialing, presumably to track down their dad.

CHAPTER SEVENTEEN

RODRIGO

With Sofia off doing who-knows-what, it's just me and Petra again. She turns to me, "So, annoying people is a hobby of yours? And here I was, thinking I was your special project."

"You? Special? Bird, I stopped putting you on a pedestal ages ago." *Probably shouldn't say it like that.*

Petra takes a deep breath, trying to keep her calm. "Good to know," she replies, her smile a confusing cocktail of bitterness, pain, or maybe just sarcasm.

Deciding to keep the ball rolling, I lean in. "If it makes you feel any better, it's mostly you and my sister who get the best of my annoying talents. Everyone else is safe from my charm."

"And what a charm it is."

"Do your eyes get tired from all that rolling?"

She shoots back, "Do your lungs ache from all the smoking?"

"Touché. Rude, but fair. And here I was, just trying to make small talk."

"Small talk with me? What's next, Rodrigo? You going soft on me?"

I shrug, "What's a guy to do when stuck with someone as 'charming' as you?"

A faint smile plays on her lips. "Charming? I'm sure that's exactly the word you had in mind."

Deborah slides into the seat next to Petra, their arms brushing. I find my gaze locked on Petra. She's stunning tonight, more than usual. That dress, her lipstick – it's not her usual style, but damn, it suits her. Trying to snap out of it, I turn my attention to my mom who settles beside me, and Pedro takes his spot opposite Deborah.

I notice Sofia's absence and lean towards Pedro, "Where's Sofia?"

Pedro glances at our mom before whispering, "Bathroom. And Dad's not coming. Sofia bolted right after the call."

Understanding Sofia's mood, I straighten my shirt and head towards the restrooms. At the ladies' room door, I knock lightly. "Sofi? You in there?" I use the old nickname, hoping it'll coax her out.

Silence.

"If you don't answer, I'm barging in. Ladies' room or not, I'm immune to gender norms," I tease, hoping to lighten the mood.

I wait a beat, then push the door open. There's Sofia, a crumpled figure on the floor, her face buried in her hands.

"Hey," I say softly, squatting beside her. "You okay?"

She looks up, eyes swimming with tears. "Dad bailed. On Pedro's birthday. Too busy for his own son," she chokes out.

I sigh, resting a hand on her shoulder. "I know, Sofi. Dad's always been... complicated."

She's wiping away tears, "Why does work always win over us?"

"Yeah, Mr. Gomez can be a real piece of work. Sorry he's dragging you into this mess now."

Mom elaborates, her smile growing. "Deborah and Pedro met the same night you and Petra did."

Shit. I see where this is headed.

Deborah, all innocent, chimes in. "Yeah, we all crashed a party together. Petra was my wing woman, and Rodrigo was Pedro's."

Mom's eyes dance between Petra and me. Petra's face is a picture of pure panic.

"Yes, it was quite the night," Petra manages, forcing a smile.

Mom lays it on thick. "My boys do pick wonderful women."

Petra's mortified. I decide to stoke the fire. "Ah, but there's nothing going on between Petra and me, right, Bird?"

Petra looks like she wants the ground to swallow her up. "Yes, absolutely nothing."

Mom's not buying it. "Oh, you two would be adorable together. The chemistry is definitely there."

Petra's eyes are screaming SOS, but I just grin and shrug. "Who knows where life will take us."

Petra's foot connects with my shin under the table. *Ouch*. But I can't wipe the grin off my face.

"Just admit it, Bird," I taunt. "Just confess you're head over heels for my charm."

"Again — in your dreams, Rodrigo." She forces a smile.

Deborah's trying to stifle her laughter, and Pedro's watching us with an amused, knowing look.

"We'll just have to agree to disagree," I say, laid-back.

Mom jumps in. "I'm putting my money on 'it's only a matter of time.'"

Petra's blushing, and I laugh.

Petra shoots back, "I'm not easily swayed."

Mom excuses herself to the restroom. "Keep enjoying the banter, kids."

As she leaves, Petra leans in, her voice tense. "What's the fuck are you doing?"

Pedro joins in, "Yeah, do tell."

I lean back, all ease. "Just stirring the pot. Your reactions are too good."

Deborah nods, adding fuel to the fire. "I think you are just in denial."

Petra throws her hands up, surrendering. "Fine, play it your way. We'd be the power couple of the century."

I chuckle, loving every second of this. "Finally, Bird sees the light."

"Sure, Rod. We're a match made in heaven. Or hell."

She's back to calling me Rod.

—

PETRA

I'm mentally plotting Rodrigo's slow and painful demise. His mom now thinks we're an item – which is just what I needed. And okay, maybe I've been caught staring at Rodrigo more times than I care to admit. The guy's a distraction in human form, we all know that by now.

Post-dinner, it's Mojito time at the open bar. Deborah hooks her arm in mine, practically dragging me there. "You remember our little chat earlier? About you and Rodrigo and–" Deborah starts, but I cut her off.

"Dee, not now. I'm already on edge."

She backs off but can't resist a parting shot. "Just saying, I'm not the only one noticing the sparks."

I try to ignore her and focus on my Mojito. Strong, sweet, and dangerously smooth. Looks like I'll be downing a few of these.

Bea, drama queen supreme, joins us with a posse from the team. Hours and several drinks later – Mojitos, Margaritas, and a rogue Negroni – I'm spinning and my ankle's throbbing.

Deborah's words are a blur in my ear. I see her and Bea heading back to the bar, probably for round who-knows-what. I lean against the wall, trying to ease my ankle.

"How many drinks in are we?" Rodrigo's voice cuts through my fog.

"Two Mojitos into 'none of your business,'" I shoot back with a tipsy shrug.

"Maybe time to hit the brakes, huh? Don't want to overdo it."

I snap, "Don't start playing 'dad' with me, Rodrigo. I know what I'm doing."

But as I push off the wall, pain shoots through my ankle, contorting my face.

Rodrigo's right there, his frustration giving way to something softer, more intense. His scent, a blend of something woodsy and undeniably masculine, wraps around me, intoxicating and overwhelming. I look away, but he lifts my chin to force eye contact.

"Let's drop the act, okay?" His voice is a low rumble, filled with unmistakable concern. "You're hurt, and those drinks aren't helping. High heels and tequila shots are a dangerous combo."

His unexpected worry catches me off guard, and I push against his chest, trying to create distance. "I said I'm fine, Rodrigo. Back off."

But he's unyielding, his hands steady on my waist, anchoring me. "Not a chance," he murmurs, his breath a warm caress against my ear. "Let's get those spare shoes from Pedro's car. I remember you mentioning them."

I'm momentarily stunned, both by his recollection and the electricity that zips through me at his touch. "Keys, Rodrigo. I don't have them," I manage to say, my thoughts racing as fast as my heart.

Rodrigo fixes me with a look before a rogue smile teases his lips. "I'll get the keys from Pedro," he says, his fingers brushing my hair back with a touch that lingers just a second too long. His gaze drops to my lips, sending a shiver through my body before he's off, leaving me leaning against the wall, my ankle still throbbing but my mind now racing with something else entirely.

He's back in a flash, dangling the car keys. "Ready for the great shoe rescue mission?"

"They're boots," I correct him.

He raises an eyebrow, "You brought boots to replace boots?"

"Dr. Martens," I clarify, feeling absurdly defensive.

Rodrigo just nods as he leads me to Pedro's car.

At the car, he rummages in the trunk and triumphantly presents my boots. "Behold, the glass slipper of the 21st century!"

"Thanks, Prince Charming. Missing your white horse?"

He ignores me and asks, "Ready to storm the castle?" Leaning against the car, that wicked glint back in his eyes. "Or are you planning a stealth escape with your knight in not-so-shining armor?"

My heart skips a beat, and I try to keep my voice steady. "Tempting, but I think surviving a night with you is already pushing my luck."

His smirk grows wider. "Is that a challenge, Cinderella?"

I don't even try to hold my smile as I slip on the boots.

He offers me a hand, and as our skin meets. I play it cool, standing up. "Let's go before Deborah sends out a search party."

"She'd probably thank me for kidnapping you for the night."

"Careful what you wish for. Now that I think of that, an escape away from drunk Bea doesn't sound so bad."

As we start to walk back, he suddenly stops and turns to me, "What if I told you I wouldn't mind being your escape?

Our eyes lock, and the world seems to fade away. The air between us crackles with unspoken tension. I swallow hard, my breath catching.

"Rod, I—"

Just as our lips are about to meet, a distant voice cuts through the moment. "Petra! Rodrigo! Where are you guys?"

We jump apart, the spell broken. Rodrigo runs a hand through his hair, his smirk returning. "Looks like the cavalry has arrived. Shall we?"

The moment we step back inside, Deborah and Bea, clearly having a blast, corner us. Deborah, with a tipsy sway, hands me a drink that looks like a liquid mystery. Bea, her words slurring slightly, fixes Rodrigo with a giggly stare.

"Look who's here!" Bea exclaims, pointing at Rodrigo. "Should've grabbed you a drink too. What's your poison, Rodrigo?"

Rodrigo just shakes his head, "I'm on driving duty tonight," he says, shooting a glance at Deborah, who's blissfully unaware, lost in her own buzz.

His eyes flicker to the drink in my hand, "You planning to down that?"

I lift the cup with a challenging smile. "Watch me."

He leans in, his voice low. "Remember, I'm not carrying you home if you pass out."

"I'm a big girl."

"We'll see about that," he says before casually turning away, disappearing into the crowd.

—

RODRIGO

The night's winding down, and the restaurant's starting to empty. A few people are clearly past their 'happy' stage. Pedro sidles up to me with a resigned look. "Seen Deborah around?"

I nod. "Last I saw, she was leading a conga line of tipsy office gals. Petra and Bea were her backup dancers."

Pedro groans, running a hand through his hair. "Great. My beautiful, drunk, soon-to-be wife is leading a parade."

I chuckle. "Need a wingman for the rescue mission?"

"Wouldn't say no to that."

Mom and Sofia join the scene, "Everything okay, boys?" Mom asks.

"All good, Mom. Just wrangling some party animals," I assure her with a grin. "Back in a flash."

Pedro and I head towards the laughter and chaos. We find Petra and Deborah propped against a wall, in stitches over something only they find hilarious. Pedro's coaxing Deborah with the promise of a cozy bed, while Petra's now a giggling heap on the floor.

"Seriously, Petra?" I crouch beside her, offering a hand. "I see you've made friends with gravity tonight."

She glances up, her laughter fading into a curious stare. "You're here to escort me to my pumpkin carriage?"

"Something like that. Let's get you vertical."

Her attempt to stand is more a collapse into my arms. "You know, this damsel-in-distress act isn't my usual style," she slurs, still clinging to me.

"I'd say you're nailing it," I quip, trying to keep the mood light, even though every neuron is screaming at me how right she feels in my arms.

Pedro, with Deborah now semi-upright, throws a comment over his shoulder. "Bea left early. I'll get Deborah to the car. I'll wait for you there. Good luck with your handful."

"Come on, Petra," I say, trying to get her attention. "Let's go home, okay?"

Petra's gaze locks onto mine, suddenly intense. "We heading back together?" she asks. *Is that a hopeful note in her voice.*

"What do you mean, Bird?"

"Are we going home together?" she asks.

My heart does a stupid little skip. "No, you're off to Deb's. I'm flying solo."

"Oh." Her disappointment is obvious, and it tugs at something inside me I didn't even know was there.

I steer her towards the exit, grabbing her coat and bag on the way. Mom and Sofia are waiting, bundled up and ready to leave.

"Can't say goodbye without a hug," Mom gives me a warm squeeze. She turns to Petra, who's sporting the world's most unconvincing sober smile. "Are you alright, dear?"

"Yes, I'm one hundred percent all right," Petra's bright response is clearly for show. I glance at Sofia, who appears to be drifting off her feet. Another casualty of the night's festivities – she always gets quiet when she drinks.

"Let's get everyone home," I say, more to myself than anyone else. "Do you know where Pedro and Deborah are?"

"They're in Pedro's car," Mom says.

I make sure Petra's steady on her feet before I let go, then turn to Mom for a quick hug. "Night, Mom."

A peck on Sofia's cheek, and I add, "Stay out of trouble, kid."

With a cautionary, "Drive safe," to Mom, I pivot back to Petra, guiding her towards Pedro's car. But she halts, swaying slightly.

"Not feeling great," she mumbles, eyes shut.

I steady her with a hand on her waist, lifting her chin. "Nausea? You need to, you know, get it out before we hit the road?"

"I'd rather not."

"Nobody likes a puke, baby, but sometimes it's the lesser evil." I pause, realizing I just slipped in a 'baby' there. But Petra, thankfully, seems too out of it to catch it.

"I'll pass," she insists, her voice hardly above a whisper.

We resume our walk, finding Pedro outside his car, looking like he's one step away from a meltdown. Deborah's slumped inside, looking green.

Pedro gives me a desperate look. "I'm outnumbered here, man. Both our ladies are on the verge."

"Yeah, Petra's joining the nausea club."

Pedro sighs. "Looks like a long night ahead. Pray they keep it together till we're home."

Then it hits me. "Hold up, you said 'we'?"

He nods, "Can't handle the double trouble alone. I need backup, come on."

I sigh, resigning myself to the task. "Alright, let's get this caravan moving. Petra, you're with me."

She looks up, "With you?"

"Yeah, I'm your chauffeur for the night," I say, guiding her to my car. Once she's settled in the passenger seat, I add, "And please, no technicolor yawns in my car. I just had it cleaned."

CHAPTER EIGHTEEN

RODRIGO

The drive back to Pedro and Deborah's was a rollercoaster – Petra almost redecorated my car interior with her stomach contents a few times. We pulled over more than I'd like to admit before finally making it.

Crawling up the stairs, Petra swears off elevators for the night. "Keys, Bird?" I ask, watching her fumble through her bag like she's digging for buried treasure. I finally grab the bag from her, ignoring the frown she shoots my way.

After an epic search, I fish out the key from the black hole of her purse and unlock the door. We stumble into the apartment, greeted by the sounds of Deborah's not-so-silent serenade to the porcelain God.

Pedro emerges, looking like he's been through a war zone. "Deborah's trashed," he says, the understatement of the century.

I nod towards Petra, who's zoning out in the hallway. "And Petra's not exactly poster girl for sobriety, right, Bird?" Petra mumbles something about sleep. "Water might be a better idea," I suggest, but she's already heading kitchen-ward like a zombie in search of brains, leaving her stuff scattered. Before we know, there's a sound from the bathroom, making Pedro groan, and taking off running.

Sofia suddenly curses, "Fuck this shit," and I react. "Language, young lady!"

"You swear all the time!"

"But that's my prerogative as the older, wiser brother," I tease. "Now go fix that makeup. You look like you've been boxing with a raccoon."

She gasps and dashes to the mirror. "It's not that bad!" she protests, shooting me a glare. "You scared me, jerk."

"Couldn't resist. You should've seen your face!"

Her smile is reluctant but there. As she tidies up, she threatens, "I'm gonna get you back for this, big time."

I chuckle. "I'm quaking in my boots, Sis. Bring it."

Back at the table, Mom's maternal radar is on full alert. I shoot her a look that says 'let it be.' She understands, shifting her focus.

Pedro leans in. "Is Sofia okay?"

"She's getting there," I assure him. "Just had a reality check about dear old Dad."

He winces. "Let's not go there tonight."

"Got it," I agree, dropping the topic.

As dinner rolls on, the table's alive with chatter. It's a cacophony of voices, but there's Petra, her presence like a magnet. Every time our eyes meet, it's electric – this unspoken tension that I just can't shake off.

Out of the blue, Mom turns to Petra. "Petra, you've known my kids for a while, right?"

Petra, ever graceful, dabs her lips with a napkin. "Yes, I met Deborah first, and then these two troublemakers," she says, nodding towards Pedro and me.

"You all met at the same time?" Mom's got this twinkle in her eye. Alarm bells start ringing in my head.

I play dumb. "Met at the same time?"

Petra is fumbling with a water bottle like it's a Rubik's cube. I swoop in, offering to help, but she's stubborn as a mule. "No, I got it!" she insists, with that cute defiant pout.

"I was just trying to be nice, Bird. It was never your choice." I grab the bottle, twist it open, and hand it back to her. She sticks her tongue out at me in a childish retort. "Always the pain in my ass, even drunk," I tease as she clumsily pours the water, nearly toppling the glass. "And graceful as ever."

Pedro reappears, looking worn. "Deborah's down for the count. Can you make sure Petra doesn't, I don't know, fall into a coma or something?"

Petra, all independent, slurs, "I don't need a babysitter. I'm fabulous."

I chuckle, steadying her swaying form. "Sure thing, fabulous. I'll keep an eye on her, Pedro. Go tend to your lady."

He thanks me and disappears back down the hall, leaving me to handle Petra, the tipsy tornado.

Petra moves to the couch and I follow her. "Are you my new shadow?" she asks.

"Seems like it."

"Why?"

"Brotherly duties," I shrug, trying not to laugh at her dramatics. "Gotta make sure you don't turn into a pumpkin or something."

She waves me off, a queen dismissing her court jester. "I'm fine. You can go." But before she can say another word, she's bolting for the bathroom, with me right on her heels.

In the bathroom, it's a glamorous scene – Petra and the porcelain throne, a classic. I squat beside her, holding her hair back. "You know, they say puke is a symbol of true love," I tease.

Petra retorts between heaves, "Yeah, it's like a fairy tale."

"Feeling any better?" I ask, helping her up after she's done paying tribute to the toilet Gods.

"Well, at least the bathroom's still in one piece," she manages to joke.

"A real hit-and-run artist," I chuckle, amused by her resilience. "Always the comedian, aren't you?"

"Thanks," she says, a weak smile on her lips, staggering past me. At the doorway, she turns, a hint of naughty in her eyes. "You're not as evil as you pretend to be."

"I'm shattered," I send a smile her way. "Here I was, aiming for devilish charm."

Entering her room, Petra announces with dramatic flair, "Behold, my kingdom."

"You know, this used to be my kingdom. I never officially abdicated."

She looks confused. "Yours?"

"Yeah, where do you think I crashed before I bought my place? This was my sanctuary." I lean against the door frame, enjoying her surprise.

Her response is almost too easy. "So, you're the king, and I'm the queen?"

"Sounds like we're an item then," I say, watching her reaction.

She sits up too quickly, her face mixed with shock and dizziness. "NO!" she protests. "That does not make us an item!"

I smile despite my best efforts. Petra's been cracking my facade more than I'd like. "Easy with the acrobatics," I advise, sitting next to her on the bed, hands safely tucked away in my pockets. I catch her off guard with my next question. "Why are you here, Petra?" I lean in, my voice low, watching as confusion dances in her eyes.

"Huh?"

"Why'd you move in here? Last time I checked, you were setting up camp in the kitchen, but I never got the backstory."

She looks away, a storm brewing behind those deep eyes. "Nowhere else to go," she whispers, almost like a secret.

"How come?"

She swallows hard, "Parents' place," she starts. "Caleb's new girlfriend... wasn't a fan of me."

"And you just... left?"

"He asked me to," she says, a pained smile on her face.

"That's not how family works, Bird," I chide gently, reaching out to lift her chin. I want her to see the sincerity in my eyes. "You don't just disappear because someone new enters the picture." Her eyes flicker with something unspoken, and I push on, "You had just as much right to that house as he did."

Her tears start to fall, and I feel a surge of protectiveness. I wipe them away, my heart squeezing with regret.

"He doesn't deserve your tears, Petra. No one does." My voice is heavy with remorse. I'm sorry for more than just her brother's actions.

She nods, trying to compose herself. I pull back, struggling with a storm of emotions inside.

"You need some sleep," I say, maintaining a safe distance. "It's late."

Petra watches me like a hawk as I make my move towards the door. "Rodrigo," her voice is soft, but it stops me cold. It's like she's got a remote control for my heartbeat.

I turn to her, my heart pounding in my chest. "Yeah, Bird?"

She's nibbling on her lip, "Would you... stay? Just for tonight?" There's a hesitance in her voice, like she's bracing for rejection.

My mind races. Stay with her? In this room that hums with the unsaid?

"I'm not sure that's the best plan, Petra," I say, aiming for calm but let's be real, I'm anything but. Especially with those eyes of hers drilling into me like I'm the last lifeboat on the Titanic.

"Why not?" She asks, her gaze steady. "Scared you might actually care?"

That hits a nerve. "I'm not scared of anything. And for the record, I do care."

She sways a bit as she stands, sending waves of her scent my way. It's unfair, really. "Prove it, then. Stay. Show me you're not just some fair-weather knight in shining armor."

I'm practically hearing her words on loop in my head. "Petra, I..." *Words, where are you when I need you?*

She's inching closer, and I'm about to spontaneously combust. I can almost feel the heat coming off her, and her lips, don't get me started on those.

"Just tonight," she breathes out, reaching for my hand. Her touch is like a live wire straight to my heart.

I shut my eyes, like that's going to help sort the mess in my head. Every sane part of me is yelling, 'Run, man, run!' But then there's this other part, this reckless, wild part that's all in on staying.

I crack my eyes open, and there she is – hope written all over her face. And that's when it hits me – this isn't just about her needing some company. This is about me needing her, in ways I didn't even let myself dream about.

"Alright," my voice is a whisper, but it feels like I'm shouting. "I'm in. Just for tonight."

The smile she gives me then, it's like the sun coming out after a storm. "Thanks," she says, and I can feel the walls I've built up over the years just starting to topple over.

She moves closer, and I notice she's a bit wobbly on her feet. "Okay, but just to be clear," I start, holding up a finger, "We're not... I mean, I'm not going to take advantage..." I'm stumbling over my words, trying to set boundaries while my mind is going wild.

"I know," she says, her voice a gentle murmur. "I just... don't want to be alone tonight."

We sit on the edge of her bed, the air between us thick with unspoken words. She leans against me, her head resting on my shoulder – her breath is warm on my neck.

I wrap an arm around her, drawing her close. It feels natural, right even. But as she turns her face up to mine, our lips inches apart, I feel like I'm walking a tightrope.

"Petra," I whisper, my voice rough. The temptation is unbearable. "You're not... I mean, we can't..."

She nods, understanding flickering in her eyes. "I know. I'm not... I'm not fully here," she admits.

It's like a bucket of ice water over my head. Right, she's not sober, and I'm not the guy who takes advantage of a situation like this. But God, it's hard.

Her hand finds mine, fingers intertwining. There's an intimacy in the gesture that's more intense than anything physical could ever be. We just sit here, holding hands, the world outside her room fading away. It's just Petra and me, lost in a moment that feels suspended in time.

I feel her leaning into me, her body warm against mine. Every cell in my body is screaming to close the gap, to taste her lips, but I hold back.

"Petra..." I start, but she puts a finger to my lips.

"Don't," she whispers. She gazes up at me, a softness in her eyes that makes my heart skip a beat. Then, she's leaning in, her lips ghosting over mine in a whisper of a kiss that's bold and as unexpected as a thunderstorm on a sunny day.

That kiss, man, it's like a match struck in a dark room. Brief, yes, but it lights up something fierce inside me, a blaze that I'm scrambling to keep under control. I pull back, just a hair, but it's like pulling away from a magnet. My breath catches in my throat, my eyes locking with hers, searching for some kind of clue in this crazy game we're playing.

"Thank you," she breathes out, her lips curved in a shy, enigmatic smile that could mean a million things. All I know is that it's messing with my head in the best way possible.

I just nod, because what can I say? My heart's doing the samba in my chest, and my thoughts are like a hurricane. That kiss, *damn*, it's like a line drawn in the sand, a before and after moment that I can't unfeel. So here I am, sitting by her side, watching her fall asleep like some love-struck fool.

—

I'm barely awake when I hear a knock at the door. "Come in," I mumble, voice sounding like I swallowed sandpaper.

Deborah pokes her head in, eyebrow raised. "Morning, Sunshine. You look like you've been run over by a truck. Twice."

I let out a groan that could pass for a bear's growl and flop back on the bed. "Feel like it, too. Think I might've gone overboard with the drinks. My head's pounding like a drum solo."

Deborah flops down next to me. "Join the club. I'm pretty sure I'm still drunk."

"Sorry, Dee," I say, feeling a twinge of guilt. "I didn't mean to drag you into my one-woman drinking contest."

She waves it off, patting my leg. "Are you kidding? I was the ringleader! Besides, now we have the perfect excuse to be couch potatoes and binge-watch trashy TV."

That actually sounds heavenly. "Count me in. Just need to arm myself with aspirin and water first."

"I'll tag along," Deborah says, hoisting herself up. "Need to drown my hangover in aspirin and maybe find something to eat."

We shuffle to the kitchen like a pair of zombies, me trying to piece together last night's events through the fog in my brain.

In the kitchen, we find Pedro, raiding the fridge like a man on a mission. He pulls out a jar of oatmeal like he's discovered treasure.

"Morning, ladies. How're my favorite party animals today?" he asks, spoon in hand.

Deborah rubs her temples like she's trying to erase last night. "Alive. Just barely. We partied a little too hard."

I'm still trying to figure out how I even made it back. "Yeah, last night's kinda fuzzy. Can't even remember getting to bed."

Pedro grins, taking a bite of his oatmeal. "Rodrigo played your knight in shining Uber. Dropped you off."

"Rodrigo?" That's one blank I can't fill. "I don't remember that."

"Just pop some aspirin. It'll clear the fog," he advises, like aspirin is the magic cure for memory loss.

I rummage through the cabinet for the aspirin, and Deborah hands me a glass of water. "You're a lifesaver," I tell her, downing the pills.

She smiles, all empathy and no judgment. "Today's about recovery and relaxation. You in?"

I nod, more than ready for a day of doing absolutely nothing. "Sounds like a plan."

—

I'm half-asleep on the couch, Dee snuggled beside me, when the sound of the door opening jerks me awake.

"Look who's back from his superhero morning run," I tease Pedro as he strides in, all bright-eyed and bushy-tailed. "Seriously, how are you not walking dead like the rest of us?"

"I guess the early bird catches the worm."

Rodrigo strolls in behind him, decked out in joggers and a hoodie. Casual Rodrigo is a rare sight – kind of like spotting a unicorn. He catches my eye for a split second before quickly looking away and closing the door.

Deborah, half-buried in the couch, lazily waves at him. "Hey," she mumbles, her arm flopping back down like it's made of lead.

Rodrigo's husky "Hey" leads a shiver down my backbone. I force myself to focus on the TV, pretending I'm not aware of him standing right behind me. They're chatting in the kitchen, but their hushed voices are drowned out by the TV.

Deborah's voice snaps me back to reality. "Earth to Petra. You with us?" She's all curled up, her fuzzy shirt over her head like she's hiding from the world.

"Yeah, yeah, I'm here," I reply, shaking my head to clear it. "Just spaced out for a sec."

"Well, un-space. We've got serious movie marathon business to attend to. No deep thoughts allowed."

"Right, movies. Let's get this show on the road."

Pedro saunters over, messing with Deborah's hair. "How about I fetch some snacks for your marathon?" he offers.

Deborah sits up, clapping like a kid promised candy. "Snacks? Yes, please!"

Pedro chuckles. "Consider it done. Just gotta hit the bathroom first." He disappears down the hallway.

I'm suddenly aware of Rodrigo next to me, glued to his phone. He doesn't look up as he asks, "Feeling okay today?"

His voice catches me off guard. "Oh, uh, yeah, I'm good, thanks," I manage to stammer out.

"That's good," he replies, still not looking at me.

"Pedro said you brought me home last night?"

Rodrigo finally looks at me, "Don't remember?"

Before I can answer Pedro reappears, "Ready to hit the store?" he asks Rodrigo, clapping him on the shoulder as they head out.

Rodrigo shoots me an unreadable look and winks at Deborah. "See you later."

I reach for the remote and start flipping through Netflix.

CHAPTER NINETEEN

RODRIGO

It's been a whirlwind two months since I landed in Seattle. Work's been my life – meetings, deadlines, more meetings. *My social life? Nonexistent.* Even those morning runs with Pedro have become a solo act – our schedules are like two ships passing in the night.

Then there's Petra. I saw her last at the office, about three weeks back. She was perched on her desk, coffee in hand, deep in conversation. Sure, she threw me a glance, but it was back to business in a flash. I keep telling myself to stop thinking about her, but who am I kidding? Ever since that night I drove her home from my brother's dinner, she's been stuck in my head like a catchy tune.

In the midst of this chaos, Ava's been a godsend. Seriously, she's the MVP of getting our new office up and running. Two months in, and she's still at it, pulling extra hours like it's nothing. She's been a rockstar, making sure everything's on point for the arrival of the IP team. I owe her big time for her dedication.

Today's D-Day – my dad and brother are swinging by to inspect the place. And me? I'm running on fumes, thanks to a cocktail of caffeine and sleepless nights. It's probably written all over my face, but hey, show must go on, right?

"Relax, you've got this," Ava chirps up, appearing beside me as I take a much-needed smoke break before the grand tour with my dad and Pedro.

"I'm fine," I mutter, more to myself than her.

"Yeah, right. You look like a zombie. When was the last time you got some actual sleep?"

I shoot her a mock-serious look. "Hey, watch it. That's no way to talk to the boss."

Ava's been my right hand since our New York days. She was dating my best friend Jax, but when he jetted off overseas for work, she chose her career over love. Their breakup hit hard, but I promised Jax I'd keep an eye on her. When Seattle called, I wasn't sure she'd tag along, but she jumped at the chance. It's been awesome having a familiar face around, and this move's a fresh start for her too — new city, new beginnings, away from the ghosts of her past with Jax.

"Try to grab some shut-eye before your family arrives," she advises, snapping me back to reality.

"I'll give it a shot," I say, flicking the cigarette butt away and following her back inside.

Pedro and Dad show up soon after. "You look terrible, man," Pedro greets me with his usual charm.

"Thanks, you too," I quip, then quickly shake hands with my dad. Ava offers them coffee, but they pass, and she retreats to her desk.

"Ready for the grand tour?" I ask, leading the way.

Our office is a carbon copy of Dad's setup size-wise, but it's got its own vibe. The dark grey granite floor on the ground level gives it a sleek, if slightly moody, feel. But the high ceilings? They open the place up, making it feel less claustrophobic.

Upstairs, where my kingdom lies, there's everything – my office, kitchen, restrooms, and even the finance and HR departments. The layout's strategic: my team works downstairs in an open space, fostering better communication and saving a few bucks on office real estate.

Walking them through, I feel a twinge of pride – this is my domain now, and despite the sleepless nights, it's shaping up to be something special.

Strolling around the upper floor, I give Dad the lowdown. "The IP team's setting up shop downstairs in the open space. Ava's the first face they'll see, handling visitors and clients. Up here, it's just HR and Finance, each with their own digs. And yeah, only the department heads and yours truly get private offices."

"Looks like you've got it all figured out." My dad says.

"The office is good to go, just waiting for the team."

Pedro chimes in. "Got anyone you need to catch up with soon?"

"Definitely the formal team. Need to get the lowdown on everything."

Pedro's eyes twinkle, "Especially Petra, right? She's the go-to for case tracking."

I play it cool. "Yeah, sure. Tell her to swing by, bring anyone else she thinks should tag along."

As we head downstairs, Dad stops me with a call. "Rodrigo, remember our deal. Stick to it."

I shove my hands in my pockets, shooting back, "I always keep my word, Papá. That's what sets us apart."

Back on the ground floor, Ava's at her desk, all business. "Need anything?"

"Actually, yeah. Can you get a schedule going for Finance and HR? Split their time between here and remote work?"

"You got it," she says, already typing away.

"Thanks, Ava."

—

PETRA

"Ms. Smith," Mr. Gomez starts, his voice steady as I step into the office, following Pedro's summon. "Rodrigo's set up in the new office. He wants you over there. Needs the 411 on all the open cases and clients before the IP team settles in."

Pedro jumps in. "Rodrigo mentioned you can tag anyone along from the team if it helps."

I muster a cool smile, my insides doing 'merry go round'. "Got it. I'll see if bringing someone along makes sense. Is there anything in particular that Rodrigo wants me to focus on?"

Pedro shakes his head, "Not that I'm aware of. Make sure you are prepared to discuss all the current cases and projects with him. He wants to get a handle on everything as soon as possible."

"Sure thing," I nod, "I'll go there after lunch. Need to let anyone know I'm coming?"

Pedro rubs his neck, "Uh, we kinda missed getting his assistant's number. But no sweat, I'll buzz him. Does that work?"

"Perfect," I say, a nervous sensation creeping up. "Could you text me the address? Need to set up my GPS."

"Coming right up," Pedro grins, all friendliness and no clue about the storm brewing inside me.

"If that's all," I say, "I'll prep for the meet downstairs."

Mr. Gomez, buried in paperwork, looks up briefly. "Appreciate it, Ms. Smith." I turn on my heel and head back to my desk.

For the next hour, I'm knee-deep in case files and project notes, prepping for my showdown with Rodrigo. When lunchtime hits, I grab my trusty laptop and a jungle of sticky notes, dashing out to my car. I'm flying solo today, no backup from the team even though the idea of being alone with Rodrigo has my stomach turn.

Lunch is at this swanky Japanese joint, me versus a poke bowl loaded with braised salmon. I'm flipping through my notes for what feels like the millionth time, anxiety nipping at my heels. What if I blank out in the meeting? Picture it – me, standing there, deer in headlights, while Rodrigo throws shade my way.

Not today, universe.

Shaking off the nerves, I focus on chowing down. I'm prepped and pumped. I've got this.

Deep breaths, Petra, deep breaths.

Lunch done, I'm off to Rodrigo's lair, trying not to trip over my own feet as I strut in.

Parking right in front of the building, I'm greeted by its towering, modern glory. Nerves start their dance routine in my stomach. *Deep breath, Petra.* Time to show them what you're made of.

The lobby's a high-end scene – black leather, sleek greys. Only company? The receptionist. She's all waves of blond hair, freckles, and eyes so blue they're almost see-through.

"Hi! Petra Smith. Here to see Rodrigo."

"Right away, Ms. Smith," she chirps, her fingers dancing over the phone. "Rodrigo, Ms. Smith has arrived." A pause. "Will do. Thanks." She hangs up, all smiles. "He'll be here in a second."

As I take in the fancy digs, Rodrigo descends the stairs. No blazer today – just a black shirt, grey trousers that stop just above the ankles, and shoes so sharp they could cut glass. He's a walking, talking GQ cover.

His approach sends my heart into overdrive. Messy yet perfect hair, those intense green eyes...

Focus, Petra, for fuck's sake.

"Thanks, Ava," Rodrigo says to the receptionist.

Ava. So, this is Ava.

"Ready?" Rodrigo's voice snaps me back.

"Yep," I manage, my smile tight. I give Ava a polite nod and trail after Rodrigo.

——

RODRIGO

Alright, I need to focus. But damn, every time she speaks, it's like my brain decides to go on vacation. And her outfit today? It's like she's personally challenging my self-control. I mean, come on! That top hugs her in all the right places, making it an impossible task to keep my thoughts G-rated.

I'm hanging onto professionalism by a thread here, but every word out of her mouth is a distraction. It's not just what she says – it's how she says it. That voice of hers, smooth and confident, it's weaving around my head, leaving me dizzy. And her eyes, damn, those eyes. They're like deep pools I just want to dive into and forget the world.

Somehow, and I mean by some freakin' miracle, we're getting through this meeting without me making a complete fool of myself. I'm internally cheering, 'Way to go, Rodrigo, you haven't embarrassed yourself... yet.' And then she asks me about the IP team, and her voice just slices right through all my thoughts. It's like a velvet knife – soft but damn sharp.

"Rodrigo, when do you want the IP team to come in?" Petra's voice cuts through my thoughts.

I seize the opportunity to tease. "I figured you'd want more of this delightful one-on-one time, Bird."

She gives me a 'you've got to be kidding' look. "Trust me, we've had our fill of alone time today."

"But you chose to come solo, right? Wanted an exclusive audience with me?" I can't resist the urge to glance at her lips

Her reply is swift and sharp. "I came alone because we had a mountain of work, not for some fantasy rendezvous you're dreaming up."

"I can dream, can't I? But don't worry, I'll let Pedro know the team's welcome anytime," I assure her. "Gotta review some urgent cases, maybe bring in some of the crew for brainstorming."

"Will you need me around for the early stages of the project?"

I blurt out without thinking, "I need you around all the time." Great, Rodrigo, real smooth. "In a strictly professional sense, obviously."

"Nice save. Saying you need me without really saying it."

I'm backtracking fast. "Just in the office! For work stuff, nothing else!" I'm aiming for stern, but I'm not sure if I'm convincing even myself.

She's skeptical but starts to pack up.

I can't resist one last jab. "Admit it, you've fantasized about being needed by me."

She stops, turns, and gives me that look. "Maybe in another lifetime. But not now."

"Your eyes are telling a different tale."

Quick as a whip, she fires back, "Seems you were the one too busy admiring the view to even look at the documents."

She noticed my wandering gaze? *Fuck.*

Before I can come up with a clever comeback, she's at the door, throwing a sly grin my way. "Just so you know, I can play this game too." And with that, she leaves the room.

I watch her leave, and let me tell you – Petra's good at this game, better than I expected.

I'm pretending to focus on work, but my mind is a total mess, all thanks to that woman. That sharp tongue of hers, the confident way she moves, and how she bats away my flirty comments like they're pesky flies, yet somehow leaves this lingering question mark in the air.

One second she's all business, the next she's firing back with a zinger that leaves me reeling. It's like she's playing chess while I'm stuck playing checkers. And the worst part? I can't stop thinking about what my next move should be.

Seriously, Petra Smith is one complex riddle wrapped in a mystery, and I'm sitting here like some lovesick detective trying to crack the code. It's ridiculous.

—

PETRA

Exiting the building I whip out my phone and call Pedro. "Hey," Pedro greets me. "How'd it go with Rodrigo?"

I feel my cheeks heat up, thinking about our back-and-forth. "Productive," I manage, "He's planning to get the IP team over to the new office. He'll fill you in. Something about checking cases with tight deadlines."

"Got it," Pedro says. "I'll chat with him."

"Awesome."

Then Pedro's all, "You good?"

I take a deep breath, steadying myself. "Yeah, I'm good. Just... it's a lot, you know? This whole setup's complex." I chuck the paperwork and my laptop in the passenger seat and hop into the driver's seat. "Heading back to the office now."

"See you soon," Pedro says.

I hang up and drive back to the office. As soon as I arrive Bea's all over me like a rash. "Spill the tea on the new boss," she demands, practically vibrating with curiosity.

"Bea, it was just boring work stuff," I say, trying to dodge her.

She gives me the puppy eyes. "You can't tell me there wasn't any sizzle between you two. His abs are like sculpted marble. There had to be something!"

"Oh my God, Bea," I say, "We talked business. That's it. And why are you so fixated on his abs?"

"I'm calling your bluff. There was definitely a spark at Pedro's birthday. And those abs? They're legendary. You can practically see them through his shirts."

I chuckle as I settle in at my desk. "Bea, there was no spark. Can we drop it now?"

"Okay, okay," Bea concedes, throwing her hands up. "But if you guys end up together and have gorgeous babies, I'm calling dibs on godmother."

I shake my head at her wild imagination. "Bea, you're getting way ahead of yourself. But I'll keep your godmother bid in mind." With a cheerful clap, Bea finally gives it a rest and heads back to her desk.

Settling at my desk, I'm supposed to dive into work, but my brain has other plans – replaying every moment of that meeting with Rodrigo. His cheeky banter, the tension, and those not-so-subtle, oh-so-frustrating stares. Why does he have to be so... infuriatingly Rodrigo?

Just as I'm about to refocus, my phone buzzes, jolting me. It's Pedro, "Rodrigo says you guys had a good meeting. Thanks for handling it."

I reply to Pedro, "No worries. We covered a lot of ground. Catch up tomorrow?"

Back to my computer, I'm trying to focus, but it's like my brain's stuck in Rodrigo mode. I can't shake the memory of his smirk, his teasing, the way he leaned in–

"Earth to Petra," Bea's voice slices through my thoughts. "You've been zoning out for ages. Everything cool?"

I blink back to reality. "Yeah, just deep in the IP cases," I say, a bit too quickly.

CHAPTER TWENTY

PETRA

Another week zips by, and Rodrigo's been like a busy bee, buried in work. He's summoned half the office to join his review-a-thon. Me? I've been dividing my time between his office and his father's office, but we hardly have time to even acknowledge each other's existence. It's like we're always running in opposite directions.

And Ava, oh boy, she's practically glued to Rodrigo. Everywhere you look, there she is – chatting him up, sharing lunch, you name it. Seriously, how much Ava-time does one man need?

Sure, she's his right hand or whatever, but this is next level. She's like his shadow, stuck to him 24/7. It's not like I'm counting, but 'Mr. No-Strings-Attached' and 'Miss Perfect Blue Eyes' are getting cozy enough to make a rom-com jealous. Here I thought Rodrigo was a hit-it-and-quit-it guy, but maybe he's eyeing a hit-it-and-put-a-ring-on-it scenario. For all I know, I might be RSVPing to their lovefest any day now.

Then out of nowhere, Rodrigo's voice booms from the stairs, "Petra," I almost leap out of my skin. Did I just think too loud?

Dropping papers, I'm a total mess. "Uh, yeah?" I squeak, scrambling to gather my dignity and the papers, hiding my flushed face.

"Got a sec to chat?" he calls down, standing there like some Greek God at the top of the stairs.

"Uh, sure," I say, smoothing down my dress, trying to look less like I've been hit by a hurricane of emotions. "Be right there." I head up, following him into his lair, I mean, office.

And there she is, Ava, sitting pretty as a picture. Fantastic, what's next? Their wedding announcement right here in his office?

"Mind shutting the door?" Rodrigo's voice is a soft command. I comply, my stomach twisting into knots.

Ava's perched in front of Rodrigo's desk, tossing me a half-hearted smile before staring back at her lap. Rodrigo, all tall, dark, and brooding, leans against his desk.

"I wouldn't normally ask this," he starts, and I'm all ears. Rodrigo's spiel begins. "Ava came from New York with me. Trusting people isn't my thing, but Ava, she's different." There's a tinge of something more in his voice.

So, they're like some modern-day Bonnie and Clyde?

"But," he continues, "Ava's boyfriend had an accident back in New York. She needs to go, take a break."

My heart races. Boyfriend? Accident?

"Jax's my best bud," Rodrigo adds, looking torn. "Wish I could go, but Seattle's got me chained."

I nod, trying to process the avalanche of information. "How can I help?"

"Dad and I have a deal about shifting team roles. I'm not looking to shuffle the deck here, but..." He takes a step toward me, and I feel the intensity radiating off him. "I need you. Like, really need you."

He's not throwing his usual flirty lines or smirks. This is Rodrigo in rare form — all business, all desperation.

"I would like to count on you to take on some of Ava's responsibilities, and not as a glorified phone-answerer or door-greeter. I need you to help steer this ship. Think managing schedules, keeping tabs on our projects..." He runs a hand through his hair, a gesture of frustration, or maybe it's vulnerability. "I need someone to manage my madness, keep the projects on track, the schedules tight." His eyes lock onto mine, like he's silently pleading.

I'm speechless. This is huge. "Rodrigo, I—" I start, but he cuts in.

"I'm lost without you, Bird," he confesses, eyes sealed on mine, a rare vulnerability showing through. "I'm not great at admitting I need help, but here I am. You're the one I trust." He pauses, searching my face. "I'm not trying to overstep, but you've got the skills, Petra. It's not so different from what you're doing now, just with a bigger picture in mind."

"Rodrigo, it's not that easy," I am definitely feeling the weight of his request.

"I'll make it worth your while," he's quick to offer.

I press my fingers against my temples, feeling a headache brewing. "Rodrigo, it's not the money that's the issue." I pause, trying to find the right words. "It's the weight of it all. The responsibility, the pressure – it's a lot. I'm not sure I'm cut out for this."

Rodrigo exhales sharply, "Just think about it, okay? Honestly, you're the only one I trust to not drop the ball here."

I'm a tangle of nerves, my thoughts racing. Glancing over at Ava, who seems lost in her own world of worry, I muster a faint, "I'm sorry, Ava." Then, without another word, I slip out of the room, leaving them behind.

I'm totally in over my head. Sure, juggling Rodrigo's schedule and all his work stuff? Piece of cake. But being glued to his side every single day? That's like walking a tightrope without a net. And I've got this inconvenient little crush on the guy that is not just messing with my head – it's doing the cha-cha on my professional integrity.

Finding out Ava wasn't his girlfriend, though? Honestly, it was like someone handed me a winning lottery ticket. But then, guilt crashes the party. How messed up is it that my first thought was, 'Yes! She's taken, but not by Rodrigo'? The guy she's with had an accident, for fuck's sake, and here I am, doing mental cartwheels.

Why do I even care? It's infuriating. I hate that I like it when Rodrigo calls me 'bird.' It's like he's got this special nickname just for me. And the way he looks at me – it's like he's trying to read my mind, or maybe undress me with his eyes. Ugh. Now I've got to work with him up close and personal. Every. Single. Day.

The worst part? Rodrigo and I, we have history. A history he seems to have conveniently forgotten. He waltzes back into my life like he didn't turn it upside down once before. And my brain? It's like it's got amnesia, just playing along with his little game. I'm at the mercy of my own runaway feelings, and it's driving me up the wall.

I can't even vent to anyone. Our past is like some top-secret CIA file – nobody knows. Deborah's in the dark, I hope… And Pedro? Well, I'm not sure, but I'm also not keen on testing those waters. So, who do I turn to for advice? Looks like it's just me, myself, and I.

Trying to dive back into work at my desk is like swimming through molasses. I'm scrolling through emails, pretending to be focused, but who am I kidding? Then, out of the blue, there's Ava, standing right in front of me. "Step outside with me?" she asks.

"Ava, I'm not really sure what to say to Rodrigo yet—" I start, but she cuts me off with a wave of her hand.

"Hey, no pressure. I'm not here to play messenger. Just wanted a chat, if that's okay?" She gives me this gentle smile, the kind that makes you feel like you're talking to an old friend.

"Sure," I reply, a little hesitant. I stand up, sending my chair rolling back with a clatter.

We stroll out to the back of the office, finding our way to this cozy little nook where folks usually hang out for smoke breaks or to escape the office buzz. Ava plops down on a bench, patting the spot next to her.

"Jax and I were an item back in the Big Apple," Ava starts, her voice tinged with nostalgia. "He and Rodrigo were buddies from their days in Spain, and when Rodrigo set up the company, Jax got on board, and that's how I landed the job there. We became this tight-knit trio, you know?"

I just nod.

"You're probably wondering why I'm dumping all this history on you," Ava continues, her eyes meeting mine. "But I think you deserve some context, especially if you're even thinking about taking Rodrigo up on his offer."

She offers a bittersweet smile.

"My career always came first, even over Jax," she confesses, her smile fading. "When he decided to jet off for work, I couldn't just up and leave with him. That's where we hit our dead end."

I open my mouth to say something, but Ava keeps going.

"Anyway, Jax was heading back to New York when this awful crash happened. He's in the hospital, and I've got to see him. Rodrigo's dying to be there too, but he's stuck here." Her eyes well up, and she quickly brushes away a tear. "With me gone, Rodrigo's kinda like a ship without a compass. He's not big on trust, so he wouldn't just let anyone fill my shoes... except for you."

"Why me?"

Ava lets out a small, sad laugh. "Why you? Because, Petra, you're different. Despite everything you guys have been through, he still trusts you more than anyone."

I freeze. "Wait, how do you know about...us?"

Ava gives me this warm, knowing smile. "He talked about you a lot when he first hit New York. No names, just this story about a girl he screwed things up with. But when I saw how he looked at you in the office, I put two and two together. Plus, the 'bird' nickname? That's not Rodrigo's style. He's not into relationships or nicknames. But with you, it's like he's hit some kind of crossroads."

I don't know what to say. I certainly wasn't expecting this.

"You know, he never actually used your name," she tells me, her voice all casual, like she's talking about the weather and not my tangled past with Rodrigo. "He'd just call you 'the most beautiful girl in the world' whenever someone asked about you. And he'd compare everyone to you — like you were this beacon of... I don't know, perfection? He always said you had a knack for making everything better."

I'm trying to wrap my head around this. Rodrigo and his cryptic ways are like a puzzle with half the pieces missing.

Then she drops another Rodrigo tidbit. "He knew about Douglas." Of course, he did. It explains that weird vibe at

Deborah and Pedro's place a few weeks back. Rodrigo's got his fingers in every pie, it seems. "And you know? He was a big part in me and Jax getting together." Ava continues, "Always telling us not to be idiots like him, to not mess up good things."

I'm trying to piece it all together, but it's like fitting square pegs in round holes. Rodrigo's actions, his words – they're a jumbled mess in my mind. He made his choices, and he decided to leave me out of the equation.

It was his call, never mine.

—

RODRIGO
THREE YEARS AGO – NEW YORK

Sitting at the bar, nursing a whiskey, I'm deep in conversation with Jax. The dim lighting of the place throws shadows around us, almost like they're swaying to the background music. I lean in closer to Jax, the memories surfacing. "You remember that girl from Seattle I mentioned before?"

But let's rewind a bit.

Earlier today, I had this unexpected heart-to-heart with my brother. See, I stumbled upon a photo of Petra with some guy, and it looked a bit too cozy for comfort. Not that it's any of my business, but there I was, getting all twisted up about it.

"So, who's the guy Petra's hanging out with in the picture she posted?" I had asked, trying to sound as casual as it gets. Pedro, with his ever-so-sharp senses, picked up on my tone.

"Why the sudden interest in Petra's social life?"

I hesitated, then figured, what the hell. "Look, there's something you should know about me and Petra," I started. My confession poured out, everything from the secret glances to the stolen moments, all the way to the deep connection we'd formed.

Pedro listened, "That's why you two suddenly stopped talking before you left for Spain? Man, I thought that was ridiculous. It makes so much more sense now."

Yeah, it did. Petra and I, we'd been this unresolved symphony, a melody that had been abruptly cut off.

So, there's that. *Pedro knows.* If he will tell Deborah about it? That's something I won't try to find out.

And now, here I am, sitting with Jax, bringing up old stories about a girl who was so much more than just a 'girl from Seattle.'

"The mysterious no-name girl?" Jax asks me with a grin, his eyes twinkling in the low light as he sips his drink.

"Yep, that's the one," I say, watching the whiskey dance in the glass.

"So, what's up with her?" he leans forward, all ears now. The curiosity in his voice is as clear as the clink of our glasses.

I take a deep swig of my whiskey, placing the glass back on the bar but keeping my grip on it, like it's some sort of lifeline. "Caught a glimpse of her on Instagram, cozying up with some dude." My voice trails off.

Jax raises an eyebrow, his interest clearly piqued. "Just friends, or...?"

I shake my head, taking another gulp, the liquid courage not quite doing its job. "Nope. Did some digging.

My brother confirmed it – they're an item." There's a bitterness in my tone, one that I can't quite hide.

Jax, ever the instigator, swivels to face me, his body language all too telling. "First off, why's she still on your Insta feed?"

I give him a dry look, "Never hit unfollow. Guess she didn't either."

"And second," he leans in, a sly smile playing on his lips, clearly enjoying this too much. "Why's it eating at you that she's with someone else?"

"Oh, cut the crap, Jax. You know exactly why."

He leans back, feigning ignorance, a master at playing the devil's advocate. "Humor me. Pretend I don't and spell it out." His teasing smile is like a red flag, and I'm the bull, all riled up.

I signal the bartender for a refill, my mind racing, not ready to dive into this conversation. "No," I say flatly, avoiding Jax's gaze.

"Dude, come on," Jax's tone turning serious, like he's about to lay down some hard truth. "You are still in love with her."

I cut him off quickly, trying to keep the walls up. "Never said that."

He ignores my interruption, "It's tough seeing her with someone else, right?" I don't bother arguing this time, knowing there's no point. The truth is as clear as the glass in my hand. "But let's be real, you pushed her away first," his voice is steady, like he's stating a fact rather than giving an opinion.

"It's not that simple," I mutter, staring ahead, my eyes fixed on some invisible point in the distance, avoiding the truth in his words.

"Actually, it is," Jax insists, turning fully towards me, his face illuminated by the dim light. "She was into you. You could've been together–"

"We couldn't, Jax. It wasn't possible."

Jax's voice rises, matching my intensity. "As I was saying before you rudely cut me off, you could be in a relationship right now. But you chose not to. She's moved on, man. You gotta live with the consequences of your choices."

Okay, now I'm annoyed. Really annoyed. "Some friend you are..."

"Exactly, I am your friend," he shoots back, "And you needed to hear this. There's a lot more I could say, you know."

I reply sharply, "No thanks."

Jax smirks, a knowing look in his eyes. "Ava would definitely have a piece to say on this."

I groan, the mere mention of Ava enough to add to my growing headache. "Oh God, not Ava. If she joins this conversation, I'm toast."

Jax chuckles, "Yeah, you'd be in deep trouble, buddy."

———

Stumbling into my apartment after a night of drowning my thoughts with Jax, I find myself in the quiet embrace of my New York pad. It's Saturday night, the city's still buzzing, but here I am, staring out of my living room window, feeling like I'm a world away from all that energy.

I toss my shoes aside, their thud against the hardwood floor echoing in the silent room. My hand's already itching for my phone as I head to the bathroom, drawn to the masochistic ritual of social media stalking. "Classic masochist move," I murmur, as I pull up Instagram and punch in Petra's handle. The familiar pang of... something, hits me as her profile loads.

There's that photo again. Petra, all smiles, cozying up to Mr. Hazel Eyes and Light Brown Hair. *She's avoiding repeat performances in her life, clearly.* But something about this guy doesn't sit right with me. His smile is a little too polished, his arm around her a little too posed. She deserves... well, someone better.

Not me, not him. *Just better.*

I end up scrolling through the rest of her photos, lost in the digital sea of her life. It's like a digital Petra Museum — each image perfectly staged, a testament to her meticulous nature. It's so very Petra — a perfectionist through and through. There's pics of her with Deborah, Pedro, her brother, some solo shots, and... oh, there's one with me. A snapshot from a time when things were simpler, more honest. She hasn't scrubbed that from her feed. I stare at it longer than I should, the ghost of a smile tugging at my lips.

The alcohol buzz warns me I'm dangerously close to doing something stupid, like firing off a regrettable message to Petra. I lock the phone with a heavy sigh and drop it on the bathroom counter, my reflection in the mirror looking back at me, a combination of regret and longing etched on my face.

Stripping down for a shower, I try to wash off the night and my muddled thoughts, the warm water cascading over me like a cleansing rain.

Mid-shower, it hits me — I didn't catch the name of Mr. Perfect-Hair in Petra's photo. Gotta put a name to the face, right? With a frustrated grunt, I turn off the water and reach for a towel, wrapping it around my waist as I leave the steamy sanctuary of the shower. My fingers are a bit pruney, and my hair's dripping as I snatch up my phone again, thumbing through her profile with a newfound determination.

There's the photo, the guy grinning like he's won the lottery. "Douglas." I murmur. He really does look like a Douglas, the kind of guy who wears sweater vests and talks about his 401k at parties.

CHAPTER TWENTY-ONE

PETRA
NOW

Stepping back into the office building, my heart's doing flips after Ava's mini-revelation session. I'm a bundle of nerves, but I've made up my mind.

I knock lightly on Rodrigo's door, and his voice floats out, "Come in."

Pushing the door open, I step inside. Rodrigo's lounging in his chair, but he straightens up as I enter.

"I've got an answer for you," I blurt out, trying to mask my inner turmoil with a veneer of confidence.

He looks at me, a spark of something in his eyes, "And?"

I shuffle closer to his desk, suddenly aware of how much space there is in the room, or how little when it's just us.

He's watching me, waiting.

I take a deep breath, "I'll do it," I say, "I'll help you with the scheduling, the planning..."

He leans back, surprise etching his features, "Really?"

"Yeah, really."

He stands up, a slow smile spreading across his face. "Well, I've got a whole new battle on my hands now." He steps closer, and I feel the air shift around us. "Dad laid down the law – no changes. This'll ruffle some feathers."

I nibble my lip, thinking. "Maybe I could talk to him, or Pedro?"

"You might charm my dad, Bird. But this one's on me."

"It's not like we're planning a revolution," I argue.

He chuckles, a sound that sends a tremor through me, "You don't know Mr. Gomez. 'No changes' means not even switching up his coffee brand."

Everything Ava said circles in my head, coloring how I see Rodrigo now. It's like I'm seeing him in a new light, all the anger I've harbored slowly draining away. But knowing Rodrigo? He'll find a way to stir up the storm again soon.

I back towards the door, but Rodrigo's voice stops me, "Bird." I turn, meeting that all-too-familiar grin. "Excited to be my right hand?"

"Feels more like stepping into a lion's den."

He raises an eyebrow, his usual playful spark dimmed, "You might be surprised."

Seizing the moment, I venture into personal territory. "Ava mentioned you and Jax."

He shifts, a hand slipping into his pocket in a move that's all Rodrigo. "Yeah, we go way back."

There's an awkward silence, and I break it, "Sorry, you know, about everything that's happened."

He gives me a look that's all business, but I can see the cracks. "Me too."

"He's going to be fine."

He squints at me, a bit suspicious. "What else did Ava spill?" His tone suggests he's fishing for something specific.

I flash him a smile, "Just the good friends part. Nothing juicy."

"Ava's great, but she can be an open book. I'd hate for her to—"

I cut him off, "Did she leave out some scandalous Rodrigo tales? Do share!"

"I just don't want my past adventures to be public knowledge."

"Getting all defensive? That's not how you treat a lifesaver."

His reply is flat, "You're not a lifesaver. You're a convenient solution."

My eyebrows shoot up. "Feeling the love here, Mr. Gomez."

Then, in a swift, unexpected move, he's got my wrist in his grasp. Firm but not rough, "Don't call me that. Ever," he commands, his eyes burning into mine.

"Why?" I challenge, a playful glint in my eye, not pulling away.

He releases my wrist, a dark shadow flickering across his face. "That's my father's name. I stand apart from him."

"Struck a nerve, did I? What's the worst I can do, Rodrigo?"

His eyes lock with mine, a dangerous dance of fire and ice. "Be careful, Petra. You're playing with matches."

I catch the change in how he addresses me. "No more 'bird'? Feeling formal today?"

He exhales, his gaze softening for a fraction of a second. "You're a paradox, Petra. One that's getting harder to ignore."

"Keep the compliments coming."

He moves in closer, his breath mingling with mine. "You're playing a dangerous game here, you know that?"

"And what if I am?"

He pulls back slightly, his eyes searching mine. "I'm not known for playing by the rules."

Our faces are so close now, I can almost taste his words. "Maybe I don't want you to play by the rules," I whisper, the words hanging heavily between us.

What the fuck am I doing?

Rodrigo's eyes darken, and he runs a finger gently down my arm, "You have no idea what you're doing."

I lean in, closing the gap until our lips are almost touching. "Maybe I do."

He hesitates, then abruptly steps back, his expression illegible. He turns away, but the connection remains. "I'll be calling my brother and dad about the Ava situation and inform them that I will need you to take her place for a while. But you won't be responsible for answering phone calls or handling reception duties. I will get someone else to take care of those tasks."

I push a little further. "So, no reception duties? What's your plan? Personal assistant by day, and—"

Not letting me finish he turns, a spark of something dark and alluring in his eyes. "If you knew what my 'personal assistant' role entails, you'd run the other way."

The intensity of his gaze is like a physical touch, and I find myself momentarily lost in it. But I regain my composure, throwing him one last challenging smile as I turn to leave, shooting him a daring look over my shoulder. "But Rodrigo, just so you know, I'm not afraid of a little fire."

His eyes follow me as I walk out and I feel like I've just danced on the edge of something dangerous.

—

Waking up to the annoying beep of my phone, I groggily reach over, disturbing Saskya, my snoozing in her dog bed. *Seriously, who texts at 5 a.m.?*

Blinking away sleep, I spot Ava's name lighting up the screen. Ah, right, New York's already in the throes of morning. The message is a kicker, "Jax woke up! He's not talking yet, but he just woke up."

A wave of relief washes over me, and I clumsily type back, "That's amazing, Ava. Keep me posted." My fingers feel like they're made of lead, making typos galore.

I toss my phone aside, trying to get a few more Z's.

At 9 a.m., my alarm is a cruel joke, blaring its way into my dreams. I sit up, groggy as hell, and rake my fingers through my hair. Squinting at my phone, I shoot a message to Pedro. "Yo, awake?" I swing my legs over the bed, Saskya already acting like my shadow.

In the bathroom, a splash of cold water is my desperate attempt at waking up. Drying off, my phone buzzes, Pedro's awake. "Hey, what's up?"

"Thinking about a morning jog. You in?"

His response is classic Pedro. "Was gonna skip, but for you? Sure."

I type back, "Meet in 15?" and chuck the phone on the bed. Grabbing my running gear, I get dressed, chuckling at Pedro's next text. "Make it 20. Need breakfast."

"Who eats breakfast?" I text back jokingly.

"Not all of us run on nicotine and bad decisions, man," he shoots back. Dressing up, I slip into a hoodie and lace up my sneakers.

Saskya needs her exercise too, so I decide she's joining the jog. Leashing her up, because I'm not ready for those 'dogs must be leashed' lectures, we hop into the car, cruising towards Pedro's place.

Pulling up at Pedro's, I fire off a text, "We've landed."

"Give me 10 more. Crash inside?"

I herd Saskya inside and the door flies open, revealing Pedro, toothbrush in mouth. "Man, you said 20 minutes an age ago."

Toothbrush out, Pedro grins sheepishly. "Blame Deb."

I wave him off. "Just hurry up, will ya?" Meanwhile, Saskya's off like a rocket down the hallway. "Saskya, no!"

Too late.

Peeking around, I see the bathroom light's on, Pedro back to brushing. Saskya's nudged open Petra's door with her nosy snout.

Giggles float from Petra's room, and Pedro's head pops out of the bathroom. "What's that about?"

"I don't run the show for Saskya here," I quip. "She's got her own agenda."

Pedro disappears back into the bathroom, and then there's Deborah, nudging me. "Morning, bro."

I raise an eyebrow. "Did you just 'bro' me?"

"Yep," she smirks, filling the kettle.

Petra floats in, Saskya bouncing behind her, all messy bun and pastel socks – *definitely not her usual look.*

"Who are you, and where's Petra?" I tease.

She shoots me a puzzled glance. "What now?"

"That pink ensemble. It's not very... you. Clashes with your eyes."

"Can't I wear what I want at home?" She grabs some almond milk, Saskya on her heels.

"I was under the impression your wardrobe was a strictly monochrome affair."

She spins, feigning shock. "For your information, I occasionally dabble in grey and brown."

Deborah interjects, looking at Petra, "Water's boiling. What's with the Moka Pot? Too good for instant?"

Petra's loading up the pot. "I prefer real coffee, thanks."

Deborah shrugs off. "I'll stick with my 'not tar' coffee, thanks."

Petra's mock-offended. "Excuse me?"

Deborah's grinning. "Instant's the real deal. No need for your antique methods."

Pedro and I exchange looks. I nudge him, "Intervene?"

"Nah, they've got this."

I try coaxing Saskya. "Run time?" She's unmoving.

Petra snickers. "Looks like she's voting to stay with her mommy."

I play along, "Oh, so it's a custody battle now?"

Her laughter fills the room. "You're nuts. I need coffee to keep up with this madness."

Pedro's at the door, "We're burning daylight here."

I can't help it. "Someone was busy making babies this morning instead of being ready for a run. And spoiler alert? It wasn't me."

Petra grimaces, "TMI, Rodrigo."

Deborah whirls around, half amused, half mortified. "Rodrigo!"

Pedro just raises his hands in protest.

Their reactions crack me up. "Alright, alright, I'm sorry." Saskya still hasn't budged. "Last chance, traitor." But she's all eyes for Petra. "Guess that's a no," I shrug, following Pedro out.

—

Deborah, coffee in hand, leans against the kitchen counter, eyeing Saskya at my feet. "She's really taken to you."

"And I can't resist her charm," I reply, giving Saskya a playful scratch behind the ears, eliciting an excited tail wag.

Deborah chuckles, then her expression turns pensive. "Petty, I'm kinda freaking out."

I straighten up, "About what?"

"The wedding with Pedro. We've been engaged forever and still no date, no plans."

I frown, puzzled. "So?"

"I'm worried... Maybe he's having doubts?"

"Dee, seriously? 'Cold feet' is just movie stuff."

She's earnest. "He proposed, I said yes, but then... nothing."

"You guys are solid, more than seven years strong. Life's just busy. The wedding's on pause, not canceled."

"But by now, shouldn't we be knee-deep in wedding planning? Am I going to be forever engaged without ever getting hitched?"

"Listen, if I were engaged, I wouldn't sweat it. It's not about the party — it's the commitment that counts," I say lightly. "You've got the ring, you've got Pedro. What more do you need? Worst case, hit the courthouse for a quickie wedding." I give her a playful elbow nudge.

"In your dreams! I want a full-blown extravaganza. I'm orchestrating this whole affair like a queen."

Her enthusiasm brings a smile to my face. "Don't stress. You're both just swamped right now. A perfect wedding needs perfect timing."

Her mood lifts. "How about a movie, just us girls?"

"Sounds good, but it's a trio. Saskya's in." We both laugh as Saskya wags her tail, happy to be included.

After an hour of coziness on the couch, with Saskya dozing half on me under the blanket, Pedro and Rodrigo return from their run.

"Hey," they both chime in.

"Hey," Deborah and I respond together. "How was it?" she asks, turning to them.

"Rodrigo was practically gasping for air by the end," Pedro teases.

Rodrigo rolls his eyes. "Blame the lungs, not the smoker."

Pedro starts, "If you'd quit smoking—" but Rodrigo cuts him off, "Unsolicited advice, Pedro."

"Where's Saskya?" Rodrigo looks around.

I reveal her under the blanket. "Cozy as can be, right here."

Rodrigo grins, bending down to pet her. "Missed your dad, huh?" Saskya's tail wags furiously.

I smirk. "More like she preferred our blanket fort to your sweaty run."

"She's just lazy," Rodrigo says. "Knows a good thing when she sees it."

Pedro, now in the kitchen, calls out, "Shower time for me. Make yourself at home, Rodrigo."

Rodrigo stands up. "Time to go, Sask." He gestures with his head, and Saskya obediently follows.

I'm surprised. "Just a head nod, and she's up?"

"She stayed because I let her," Rodrigo says, "She does like you, though."

"Rodrigo," I get up as he heads out. "How's Ava?"

He pauses, a softness in his eyes. "She texted earlier. Jax is awake."

"That's amazing," I reply, genuinely happy. "I've been wanting to text her but never got her number."

"You want it?" He towers over me, his height more pronounced as I'm in socks.

"If she's okay with it..." I start, but he hands me his phone, unlocked. "Smooth move, Rodrigo," I say, typing in my number.

"Just for Ava's number," he grins.

"Or you could've just told me her number."

"It's the only way, Bird." He shrugs. "I'm terrible with big numbers. Better to be safe than sorry, right?"

I hand back his phone. "You know, you could've just asked for my number."

He fakes ignorance, "Asked for what now?"

"My number. You didn't have to use poor Ava as an excuse."

"You were the one asking for her phone number."

"Hers, not yours."

"And I didn't give you my number, did I, Bird?" he holds my gaze.

"Just text me hers," I say, unable to suppress a smile, heading back to the couch.

—

Did I just use Ava to get Petra's number? Grinning like a cat who got the cream, I save her contact as 'Clumsy Bird'. It's a small victory, but it's got me feeling all kinds of smug.

With a slight shake of my head, I send her Ava's number. "There you go," I announce, sauntering over to Petra with my phone in hand. "Sent you Ava's number. She'll be thrilled to hear from you." Petra's quick to check her phone, and I sneak a peek just in time to see she's saving my number.

So, she's keeping it, huh?

She's halfway through saving Ava's number and about to text her when she catches me spying. Clutching her phone to her chest, she throws me a mock scowl. "What do you want?" she teases, shooing me away.

I can't suppress my laughter at her act. "Go on, Bird. Chat away with Ava. But hey, try not to talk me up too much," I joke, making a beeline for the door with Saskya by my side, not waiting for her comeback.

Saskya's beside me, tail wagging, still buzzing from our visit. "Adios, chicas," I call out, throwing a last glance their way as I close the door.

CHAPTER TWENTY-TWO

RODRIGO
SEVEN AND A HALF YEARS AGO

"And we really have to go to this party?" I ask Pedro, taking a long drag of my cigarette as we stroll towards some dude's house.

"Yes, Rodrigo!"

It's a chilly August night in Seattle, but here we are, heading to a bash at some guy's place – a friend of a friend of a friend of my brother's buddy. Pedro, ever the party animal, thinks there's no better way to spend a Friday night. *Me? I'm not convinced.*

I exhale a cloud of smoke. "Feels like we're walking straight into a disaster."

Pedro just laughs. "Come on, Rodrigo. When's the last time you had a bad night with me?" He grins like he's already won.

I play along, "Uh, how about every weekend?"

His laughter gets louder. "Where's your spirit of adventure, man?"

"I left it at home, tucked in with my sense of responsibility," I deadpan. Pedro just shakes his head, undeterred, pulling me along.

There's a crowd outside, the door's wide open, lights blazing. Feels like a scene straight out of a movie.

"Party's already hopping," Pedro notes, practically buzzing with excitement.

Stepping inside, I'm hit by the chaos — loud music, the stench of beer. It's definitely a party. I take a deep breath, bracing myself for whatever the night throws at me.

"So, what's the plan here?" I yell over the din.

"We're gonna have a blast!" Pedro bellows back, picking a plastic cup up at the door and going for the booze. I follow, weaving through the crowd, "And remind me why I'm here again?" I have to shout to make myself heard.

Pedro just laughs, his eyes alight with the thrill of the night ahead. "TO PARTY!" he bellows, and just like that, he's off, spotting a familiar face and disappearing into a crowd.

Great. Now I'm solo at a party I didn't even want to come to. I'm not exactly Mr. Sociable. Why did I let myself get dragged into this?

Shaking my head, I decide to grab a drink and hunt for a quieter spot. It's not that I'm anti-fun — it's just that loud, crowded parties with a bunch of strangers aren't my scene. I grab a drink from a table, not caring much what it is, and take a cautious sip.

I weave through the mob on the ground floor. This place is massive, but it's packed like a can of sardines. I double back to the entrance and head upstairs, dodging the party-goers lounging on the steps and plastered against the walls.

Upstairs is slightly less chaotic. I start scouting for a spot that's not occupied by couples making out or worse — I'm trying to avoid any unwanted anatomy lessons here.

Finally, I find a door that's ajar. I push it open cautiously, peeking inside. It looks empty. I step in, noticing the swanky red velvet couch. *Whoever owns this place is loaded.* The room is dim, just a small lamp casting a soft glow.

As I'm about to sit, a voice surprises me. "Hi!" I spin around and spot another couch, hidden from the door's view. Sitting there is a girl, probable younger than me, but definitely not a kid. Maybe twenty, twenty-one?

I pause, taking in the unexpected company – the night just got a bit more interesting.

"Hi there," I say with a chortle, caught off guard. "Didn't notice you in the shadows."

She grins, phone in hand, lounging on the couch with a casual vibe. "Hiding out too, huh?" She's a striking contrast in her outfit – a black halter top and high-waisted trousers, offset by white Nikes.

"Seems like it," I reply, still standing there like a statue.

"Take a seat," she smirks, briefly looking up from her phone. "I promise I won't bite."

I sit down across from her. "So, not a fan of the party scene?"

She glances up from her phone, a playful spark in her eyes. "No idea who's throwing this shindig."

"That's two of us," I admit, chucking my phone onto the table between us. "My brother's the social butterfly, dragged me here," I confess, leaning back.

She laughs, a sound that's unexpectedly pleasant. "Sounds like my best friend. 'It's going to be great,' she promised." Her eye roll is theatrical, but the smile stays put.

"Are you sure we're not talking about the same person?"

She laughs. "Unless your brother's named Deborah, I doubt it."

I stroke my chin, pretending to ponder. "Nope, no Deborah here."

She tosses out casually, "Petra, by the way."

It takes me a second. "Oh, Petra, like the bird?"

"I guess? I don't know much about birds." She giggles.

I let a moment pass before introducing myself. "Rodrigo," which earns me a warm smile from her.

"Nice to meet you, Rodrigo." The way she says my name, there's something about it.

—

PETRA

Rodrigo – there's a Latin charm about him that's hard to ignore.

"Plan on turning this room into your personal hideout for the night?" Rodrigo asks, thumbing through his phone, his glance fleeting towards me.

"Figured I'd lay low till Deborah starts a search party," I reply, trying for seriousness but a laugh escapes me.

"Ditching your buddy, eh?"

I return the grin. "As if you left a note for your brother – 'Gone partying with a mystery girl.'"

"Touché," he acknowledges with a nod. I take a sip of my drink, mirroring his action.

"Since we're both AWOL," he continues, putting his cup down, "How many people here do you think actually know the guy throwing this party?"

I pretend to ponder, then answer, "A generous two."

He whistles softly. "Keeping expectations low, I see."

"And you? How many party refugees do you reckon are here?" I

He laughs. "Just us. Who comes to a party to camp out in the..." He scans the room, bemused. "...library?"

"Good point." I smile and then lean forward, intrigued. "So, are you local?"

"Seattle, or America as a whole?"

"America, I guess?" A bit of heat creeps into my cheeks. *This is not your everyday conversation starter, Petra.*

He grins. "Hispanic American. Mom's from the States, Dad's from Spain. They brought up me and my siblings between Seattle and New York."

"You speak Spanish then?" I ask, genuinely interested.

"Fluently," he confirms with a nod.

"I'd love to hear some."

Rodrigo's laugh is infectious. "Eres muy bonita," he says, eyes on me for my reaction.

"What does that mean?"

He smirks. "Never said I'd play translator."

I pout slightly. "But I don't know Spanish."

"That's a shame," he replies, the smile lingering.

"Would you teach me, though?" I persist, laying on the puppy-dog eyes.

He chuckles, clearly entertained. "You want a Spanish lesson right here and now?"

I nod eagerly, "Seems like Deborah and your brother are MIA. Perfect for a Spanish crash course, right?"

Rodrigo's laugh is a melody. "Spanish lessons in a secret party room? That's one for the books."

I flash my most charming grin. "Gotta seize the moment."

"Alright, what do you want to learn?"

"Surprise me."

He leans in, "Let's kick it off easy: Encantado de conocerte." His voice is a warm whisper, and I'm hanging on every syllable.

"Translation, please?"

He grins, his eyes not leaving mine. "It means 'Nice to meet you'. But there's more to it, you know. It's not just words – it's a feeling."

My heart skips a beat. *Are you flirting with me, sir?*

"Can you repeat that?"

He repeats, slow and clear, "Encantado de conocerte."

I echo, "Encantado de conocerte," feeling a thrill as he watches me closely.

He corrects softly, "Since you are a woman, it's 'encantada' for you." His gaze is intense, making my heart race.

I beam, "Encantada de conocerte."

His laughter rings out, warm and genuine. "Nailed it."

The night zips by, filled with Spanish lessons and laughter, and our conversation flows effortlessly. We talk about everything and nothing, the world outside forgotten.

I glance out the window, noting the late hour, just as a guy bursts in. "Bro, where've you been?"

Rodrigo, unfazed, replies with a grin. "Just here, enjoying the night. Did you miss me?"

This guy is quick to say 'hi' after a brief moment. "Sorry, I'm Pedro, Rodrigo's brother."

"No worries. I'm Petra!" I reply with an easy smile as Pedro and Rodrigo share a sibling look, and I look back out the window. "Still no Deborah."

Then Deborah appears, "Where have you been?"

"Just here, enjoying the night. Did you miss me?" I respond, echoing Rodrigo's casual tone.

Rodrigo stands, his laughter infectious. "It's like a scripted comedy."

I hold up a hand as Pedro suggests leaving. "Wait, introductions first." Deborah's gaze shifts between us. "This is Rodrigo," I say with a teasing edge. "The guy I've been hidden with while you forgot about me. And Pedro, that's Rodrigo's brother. We just met."

Rodrigo gives me a knowing look making me smile.

"So, you dragged Rodrigo here, like I did with Petra?" Deborah asks Pedro.

Pedro grins broadly, puffing out his chest jokingly. "The party king, in the flesh. The man, the myth, the legend."

Rodrigo joins in, "Yeah, the 'king' who kidnaps his brother for party adventures. If only our subjects knew..."

Our laughter blends together, "Trapped by our dearest," I add.

Deborah says still grinning from ear to ear, "Let's ditch this and grab drinks?"

I shake my head, but the smile on my face is undeniable. "You and your need to socialize!"

Rodrigo, leaning slightly towards me, adopts a playfully wounded expression, whispering only for me to hear. "Tired of my company already? And here I thought we were having a romance in the making."

"I'm all for it. Lead the way, Miss Social Butterfly." Pedro cuts in.

Rodrigo turns to me, "Care to test our 'romance' in a more public setting, Señorita Petra?"

"Only if you promise to keep up the Spanish lessons, Señor Rodrigo."

His smile is all kinds of trouble. "Oh, I've got lessons for you, alright. But be prepared, I might just ramp it up to expert level."

I raise an eyebrow, "Bring it on. I'm not one to back down from a challenge, especially not from the 'party king's brother'."

His laughter is a rich sound that fills the space between us as we trail after Deborah and Pedro.

Deborah, our self-appointed leader, calls back, "Hope you're all geared up for round two. The night's far from over."

Walking next to me, Rodrigo leans in, "Think you can handle it? My classes tend to be a bit... intense."

I keep pace with him, "I'm all about intensity."

He lets out a low chuckle. "Watch out, Bird. I'm not your average teacher."

Bird. He called me 'Bird'.

From ahead, Deborah's laughter floats back to us. "Petty, looks like you hit the jackpot tonight. A very handsome tutor, and all because of me."

Rodrigo's hand goes to his heart, "Hey, let's not downplay the talent here."

Pedro opens the door for us, gesturing grandly. "After you, ladies and gentleman. Let's see if the outside world can handle our charm."

Stepping out into the cool night, Rodrigo's gentle nudge brings a smile to my face. "You know, I might have been dragged here tonight, but meeting you? Definitely the highlight of my evening."

CHAPTER TWENTY-THREE

RODRIGO
NOW

Dad's green light for Petra to fill Ava's shoes, while she's off playing New Yorker with Jax, has kinda reshuffled the deck for us. Petra and I, we're like this dynamic duo now – part secretary, part wing-woman, part 'remember when we used to...'. Our days of bickering like an old married couple? Now, it's more like an indie flick where ex-lovers are awkwardly cool.

Flashback to me hitting Seattle's tarmac. Rebooting anything with Petra was nowhere on my to-do list. I was all about jet-setting between Seattle and New York, not getting sucker-punched by old flames that decided to reignite. Feels like I'm living a greatest hits album of heartbreak – front row, VIP access.

But here's the drama – the big, glaring 'do not enter' sign. Been down this road before, had a spectacular crash landing about six years back.

Now, sure, I'm a bit more put together, got my life sort of on track – but diving back into the love pool? With a past with Petra that's stickier than superglue? *Not exactly what I had in mind.*

Every time she's in the same zip code, my body decides it's party time. Heart racing like it's in the Indy 500, palms doing their best waterfall impression, brain taking a vacation. And those eyes of hers – they're like kryptonite. Me, the resident Ice King, finding my walls not just cracking but practically getting bulldozed by her.

But then, there's the 'what if'. What if I swing the doors wide open and she's just not into the whole 'let's give it another shot' show? Would I, in her shoes, walk through that door? Considering I basically nuked our friendship to 'save' her from my own mess. It's like one of those romances where the guy messes up big time and spends the entire movie trying to fix it.

Standing at this crossroads, life's dishing out a 'choose your own heartbreak' story. Part of me wants to fix what I broke, but is it too late? The last thing I want is to be the villain in her story again.

—

PETRA

Since Mr. Gomez gave the green light for me to fill Ava's shoes, things with Rodrigo have taken a weird turn for the better. And let me tell you, *it's kind of unsettling.*

Our usual back-and-forth bickering? It's simmered down. He's not hounding me like before. But that day he left – his words, that look in his eyes – it's like a permanent marker on my brain.

Thinking Rodrigo and I might rekindle something? That's like waiting for a cactus to bloom roses. Mr. 'Relationships Aren't My Thing' made his stance pretty clear when he hopped a plane to Spain. And in those six years of nothing but crickets? We never really got into the nitty-gritty of it all. Sure, I'd sneak peeks at his Instagram, never quite managing to hit 'unfollow', but that's about it. We morphed into strangers with a shared history.

What really stings, though, is how he never reached out. Not a text, not an 'I'm sorry', nothing. Now he's back in Seattle, and it's as if he doesn't have a single ounce of remorse about how he left things.

But that's Rodrigo for you. The guy's about as open with his feelings as a clam. Stubborn, proud – it's been his MO since forever. But part of keeps wondering about those 'what-ifs'. What if he had just opened up that day instead of hitting the self-destruct button on us?

I keep telling myself, 'Girl, don't fall for it again.' But these feelings? They're not exactly toeing the line. And the thought of round two with heartbreak? *Not exactly top of my wishlist.*

"No fucking way!" I gasp, my eyes practically bugging out as I stare at my phone. Douglas is calling. *Yep, that Douglas.* My heart's doing this weird, Olympic-level gymnastics routine. I'm rooted to the spot in the office kitchen, grateful it's just me and my racing pulse in here.

It feels like forever since Douglas and I last crossed paths. And now, out of the blue, he's dialing me up? The dude who thought 'faithful' was a suggestion, not a commitment. Why's he suddenly popping up? Is there some cheaters' bat-signal I'm not aware of?

Deep breath, girl. You're stronger than this. You don't owe him a thing. You can totally ghost his call. But there's this itch of curiosity, wondering what Mr. 'Oops, I Cheated' has to say. I'm teetering on the edge of answering when – bam! – he hangs up. Talk about a sigh of relief.

Then, my phone buzzes. A text from Douglas.

Fuck, right. Texts are a thing.

I stare at that notification like it's a bomb about to go off. Finally, I cave and open it.

"I know you're probably wondering why I'm reaching out..." Oh, Sherlock's got nothing on you, buddy. "I'm sorry. I messed up, regret it every day. Wanted to apologize." Yeah, and I want a million dollars, but we can't always get what we want, can we?

He's not done – another text.

"Yara's pregnant. She misses you. We both do." Yara, his twin, and my former friend. It's not that I don't care about her, but the thought of a reunion – and possibly bumping into him – has my stomach doing weird noises.

I don't even think about hitting reply on Douglas' message. Seriously, what's the point? A year of 'us' and he runs off with Miss Bottle Blonde.

Yeah, the guy's got looks, but that's no free pass for being a grade-A jerk. And if I'm being honest? He's as far from Rodrigo as you can get, and back then, I needed someone who didn't remind me of Mr. Tall, Dark, and Complicated.

Then, another text from Douglas buzzes in. "Let's meet, please, Pet." Followed by, "Just talk. Nothing more. You, me, Yara." I'm staring at my phone like it's a puzzle with missing pieces. Should I even bother meeting Yara?

Mia from Rodrigo's finance team breezes in, yanking me out of my Douglas-induced daze. She's all smiles and morning energy.

I fire off a quick SOS to Deborah, spilling the beans about Douglas' call.

Her response is instant, "WTF? Did you pick up?"

If she could see me, she'd know I'm shaking my head. "Nope. But he's texting like it's going out of style."

"What the heck does he want now?"

Taking a deep breath, I text back, "He says Yara's pregnant and wants to see me."

"Sure, Yara..." Deborah's doubt practically jumps through the phone. I mean, she and Yara were never BFFs, but it's not like they were enemies. Another message from her pops up, "He's just using her, you know?"

"Yeah," I type, "Happy for Yara, though. Should I meet up?"

"Girl, don't be naive. Why's he the messenger?"

"Good point."

"Always right," she texts back, her words echoing in my head. "Just don't do anything dumb, okay?"

I mentally roll my eyes and shoot back, "Alright, you win. Maybe you're right."

Phone locked and back in my pocket, I refocus on work. But as I'm about to leave the kitchen, I remember the real reason I came here – coffee. I pour myself a cup, the aroma of fresh brew filling the air, then head back to my desk, ready to dive into the day's chaos.

———

I'm submerged in emails when Rodrigo strolls up to my desk, smooth as ever in his perfectly tailored get-up. He's all crisp white shirt and charcoal trousers, looking like he stepped out of a GQ photoshoot. "Bird, got a favor to ask," he says, voice low enough for just me.

"What's up?" I glance at him, then back at my screen, fingers still dancing over the keyboard.

"Can you crash with Sask for a week?" he drops this bomb, totally out of left field.

I pause, mid-type, and swivel to face him. "Why?" I ask, trying to decode his poker face.

He pulls up a chair, spins mine to face him, "Jax is finally out of the hospital. Ava's solo there. I need to be with them," he explains, straight-faced.

I notice his hands still on my chair, an inch from my knees. I look up, and he smirks, pulling away. I clear my throat, "Sure, I can hang with Sask, but... I'm bunking with Deborah and Pedro. Shouldn't you be asking them before you ask me?"

He leans back, a look on his face like he's holding back a secret. "Thing is, Deborah's not exactly thrilled with Saskya being at the apartment for a week straight. Last time, she ended up at my sister's."

Confusion hits me like a truck. "Wait, if she can't stay at the apartment, how am I supposed to watch her?"

Here comes the kicker. He closes his eyes, like he's prepping for a storm. "You'd need to stay at my place for the week."

"Your place?" I echo, making sure I got that right. This is Rodrigo's grand plan? Me, staying at his house for a whole week?

"Yep, my place," he confirms, dead serious. My mind's spinning at the thought of shacking up at Rodrigo's for an entire week.

"But didn't you say she stayed with your sister last time?"

He shrugs, all casual. "That was before the great Sofia's Dress Disaster at Pedro's birthday. Let's just say my sister wasn't exactly throwing a parade for Sask after that."

"So, let me get this straight. You want me to camp out at your house for a week?"

"That's the plan," he says, flashing that grin of his.

"Why is it always me who gets roped into your wild schemes?"

He puts on this oh-so-innocent face. "It's simple – you're at Pedro's doing the same thing you'd be doing at my house. Just move the party to my place. Sask adores you, and the feeling's mutual, right?" He's laying it on thick now, those puppy-dog eyes on full blast.

I let out an exasperated sigh, "I need to think about this—"

"No time for thinking, Bird. I'm on a tight schedule here."

"Rodrigo!" I protest. "You can't just spring this stuff on me out of nowhere."

"It's no big deal. I've got a flight early morning. I just need you to head over to my place after work – make yourself at home." He's all charm now, trying to seal the deal.

"Fine, but there better be some perks in this palace-sitting gig." I say, turning back to my computer, but before I can refocus, Rodrigo spins my chair to face him again.

"Perks? Like what? Room service? A personal butler?"

"At the very least, I expect a fully stocked fridge. And none of that health food nonsense. I want the good stuff – ice cream, pizza, the works."

He leans in closer, his voice dropping to a whisper. "Anything for you, Bird. I'll even throw in my secret stash of gourmet chocolate. But don't tell anyone – it's a Gomez family secret."

"All right, I'll do it," I say, trying not to show how his closeness affects me. "But you owe me big time, Rodrigo."

He leans in even closer, his breath warm on my ear, "Thank you, Bird. I promise I will make it up to you." As he straightens up and sets my chair back, "I'll hand over the keys tonight. But first, let's take a grand tour of Casa de Rodrigo. Gotta make sure it's Petra-approved."

I try to keep my composure, despite the fluttering in my stomach. "I'll be judging harshly. I expect nothing less than a palace."

Rodrigo winks, "Prepare to be amazed. My humble abode is the epitome of luxury. It even has the most advanced coffee maker known to mankind."

I snort, "Wow, a fancy coffee maker? You really know the way to a girl's heart."

He chuckles, "Only the best for my favorite house-sitter. You might just decide to move in."

I shake my head with a smile, "In your dreams, Gomez."

CHAPTER TWENTY-FOUR

RODRIGO

It's the end of the workday, and I've got to play tour guide to Petra at my place. I grab the keys, close up shop in my office, and head down to where Petra's buried in her work.

Striding up to her desk, I flash my best Rodrigo-special grin. "Ready to check out Casa de Rodrigo?"

Petra looks up, her eyebrows knitting in confusion. "Now? You said 'tonight'. Last time I checked, the sun's still out..."

I lean against her desk, enjoying the slight frown on her face. "In Rodrigo's world, 'tonight' means post-work. And babe, it's post-work time."

"But, as you can clearly see, I'm still knee-deep in work," she casually taps at her keyboard.

I inch closer, dropping my voice to a mock-serious tone. "And as your incredibly considerate boss, I'm here to save you from overtime. Let's roll, Bird. Saskya won't feed herself."

Petra gives me a look, "I've got stuff to wrap up, Rodrigo."

"Bird, hit the off button on that thing. We're heading home." I catch my slip-up – 'home' instead of 'my place' – but I don't correct it. Let her stew on that.

Petra sighs like I'm her most tedious chore. "Fine. But if a client's knocking down your door tomorrow, don't look at me."

"Won't be here, remember?" She pauses, a flicker of something – *disappointment?* – crossing her face. "Gonna miss me, aren't you? Don't worry, I'll be back before you start pining away."

The moment the words leave my mouth, I realize I've tread into a minefield. Petra shoots me a sharp look. "Not the first time you've left someone behind, is it? For all I know there's no certainty you'll come back." She grabs her stuff and breezes past me.

I let out a low whistle and follow her out, bidding a quick goodbye to the lingering office folks. "You do realize I've got the wheels, right?" I call out as she heads for the door.

"And you do realize I've got my own car, right?" she throws back without a backward glance.

I hustle to catch up with her, stepping in front to block her path. Gently, I reach out, taking her arm to stop her. "Wait up, Bird."

"What?" Petra shoots back, irritation lacing her voice like a hint of spice in a sweet dessert.

"How about dinner with me?" I toss the invitation out there, watching her guard drop for a split second. Her lips curl into a brief smile – *bingo*.

"Rodrigo, Rodrigo..." she drawls, her head tilting in that cute way that always gets me. "Are you actually being straight with me? No secret motives?"

"Yes or no, Bird? I'm not the kind to beg."

"It depends," she answers, wrapping her arms around herself against the chill.

"On what, exactly?"

"On your intention. Is this dinner about showing off your place, or do you really want to have dinner with me?" She's got me there, always reading between the lines.

I pause, mirroring her earlier response. "Bird, it depends."

She echoes my question. "On what, exactly?"

"On which answer will get you to say yes," I shoot back with a grin.

That cracks her up. "Touché..." she concedes, shaking her head. "Alright, I'm in – dinner it is. But you still dodged my question."

"Where to? My place or out somewhere fancy?"

She gives me a playful look. "What is this, Rodrigo? Turning into a date?"

I lean in a bit, gauging her reaction. "Do you want it to be a date?"

Her smirk falters for just a moment before returning. "Depends. Which one would be your answer?" She strides past me to her car, leaving me standing there with a chuckle.

"Touché, Bird..." I mutter under my breath. Catching up to her car, I stop by the driver's door. "Follow me. Dinner's at my place."

She nods, a smile still playing on her lips as she closes the door. "Okay."

I head to my car, firing up the engine. Petra falls in line behind me as we make our way to my house.

The drive over to my place is quick, and before I know it, we're pulling into my driveway. We hop out of our cars, and I throw in a little flair.

"Welcome to my humble abode," I announce with a bow, gesturing for Petra to go ahead. "Watch out, it might just blow your mind."

She steps inside, her eyes scanning the space like she's sizing up a rival. "Not bad."

Saskya, ever the charmer, bounds up to Petra, paws on her waist. Petra's laugh rings out, genuine and warm. "Missed you too, furball."

I lead her through the house, showing off the kitchen, the living room, then the parade of bedrooms. "Take your pick," I say, sweeping my hand around. "But feel free to crash in mine." I flash her a grin, part challenge, part invitation.

"The lengths you go to, Rodrigo. Desperate much?"

"Only for you, Bird."

She looks at me all ready to reply, but I turn around and continue with the tour not giving her a chance to say anything.

In the kitchen, I flip on the lights, leaning against the counter. "I'd whip up a gourmet meal, but let's not pretend I'm Chef Rodrigo tonight." I pull out my phone and open Uber Eats. "Your pick, or shall I surprise you?"

Petra glances from me to the phone. "Surprise me," she says, her gaze lingering on mine a moment longer than necessary.

"You got it," My lips curl into a smile as I browse the options. But then her phone buzzes, wiping that smile clean off her face. "Everything cool, Bird?"

She forces a smile, locks her phone, and shoves it back into her pocket. "All good," she claims, her attention shifting to Saskya at her feet.

I don't press further. Some lines, even I don't cross. So, I focus on picking out our dinner.

PETRA

We're crashed on Rodrigo's couch, wolfing down pasta like we've got a personal vendetta against it, and sipping on red wine as if we're extras in a Roman epic. The carbonara? Divine. It's like my taste buds are throwing a rave in my mouth. Sure, we could've gone all posh and sat at the dining table, but this? This is way better. We're sprawled out like we own the place – he does – the TV chattering in the background, but let's be real – it's just for ambiance.

In the midst of this cozy little scene, my phone decides to join the party. It buzzes, and I see Yara's name flashing on the screen. Timing is a funny thing. Deborah was right on the money – Yara reaching out personally was the real deal, not Douglas and his cryptic texts. And here she is, lighting up my phone like a Christmas tree – I don't bother replying.

I'm a pro at keeping my poker face, though. Rodrigo's clueless about the storm brewing in my head. The wine, his chill vibe, they're like a balm smoothing over the rough edges of my day.

The carbonara is a memory now, and I'm realizing maybe I flirted a little too much with the wine bottle. There's a gentle buzz in my head, and I remember I've got to head back to Deborah and Pedro's place. The whole room feels a bit swimmy, but well, it's all part of the adventure.

Rodrigo, with his annoyingly perfect smirk, parades the plates to the sink. I'm right on his heels, wine-fueled courage in tow. "I'm not totally useless, you know. Let me help with something," I insist, reaching for a dish.

He blocks my attempt with a quick sidestep. "Nah, Bird. You're a guest. Plus, I've seen your idea of 'helping'. It involves more breaking than cleaning."

I nudge him with my hip, a playful challenge. "Excuse me, I'll have you know I'm a master dish dryer. It's a highly underrated skill."

His laugh is a low rumble, the sound sending a weird flutter through me. "Alright, master dish dryer, grab a towel. But I'm warning you, break a plate and you'll be on dish duty for a week."

"Deal," I say, grabbing a towel with more bravado than I feel. That's when I clumsily bump into him, a little too close for comfort.

"Easy there," Rodrigo murmurs.

I stand there, a little dazed, my comeback stuck somewhere between my brain and my mouth.

Rodrigo leans in, the playful glint in his eyes turning into something more intense. "You know, if you wanted to get closer, you just had to say."

I'm trying to form a witty reply, but it's like he's sucked all the air out of the room.

He inches closer, his voice dropping to a whisper, "Just say 'no' if you don't want this."

My brain's yelling, 'This is a bad idea,' but my heart? It's not just on board – it's leading the charge.

Our lips meet, and suddenly, I'm not thinking anymore. All I know is Rodrigo's lips on mine, the taste of wine, and a warmth spreading through me like I'm standing in the sun. The world falls away, and for a moment, it's just us, tangled in this reckless, perfect kiss.

—

RODRIGO

"You know, if you wanted to get closer, you just had to say." I tease, my smirk plastered on, but inside, I'm anything but steady.

Her eyes are darting between mine and my lips, and there's this uncertainty in them that's got my heart doing the flips.

I'm teetering on the edge here, whispering, "Just say 'no' if you don't want this." My heart's pounding like it's trying to escape my chest. Petra's silent, her gaze locked on mine, and that's all the green light I need. I lean in, and our lips meet.

This is a whirlwind of emotion. My heart's racing, and I swear I can feel hers beating against my chest – it's like we've time-traveled back to 2016. She's not pushing me away, not freaking out. She's right there with me, kissing me back, and I'm lost in what this means.

But then, the real-world crashes in – my phone's ringing like it's got a campaign against us. It jars Petra away, and there's this hesitation on her face, like she's trying to make sense of what just happened. I fish out my phone, cursing at the unknown caller. Petra's just shaking her head, lost in her thoughts, and walks away to the living room, leaving me stranded in the kitchen like a shipwrecked sailor.

I follow her into the living room, finding her on the couch, lost in thought. "Petra—" I begin, but she's quick to shut me down.

"Don't," she says sharply, her eyes not meeting mine.

I sit beside her, trying to bridge the gulf between us. "Look... I'm sorry, okay? I'm sorry for... everything."

Her laugh is a cold blade. "You're sorry? That's rich."

"I'm sorry for making you feel whatever this is. But that kiss... I am not sorry about that."

She finally looks at me, her gaze a fortified barrier. "Suspicious, Rodrigo. That's what I'm feeling. What's your endgame here?"

"Earlier, when you asked why I wanted to have dinner with you?" I take a deep breath, diving into the truth. "The truth is, I genuinely wanted to have dinner with you. Just you."

Her bitter laugh cuts through the air. "Why, Rodrigo? Why all of this now? You left, and it seemed like you didn't care at all."

"Why did I come back?" I echo her unspoken question, feeling the weight of her stare. "I cared, Petra. I always did. I just... I was a mess at showing it."

Her facade cracks for a moment as a tear escapes her eye. She quickly wipes it away, but it's too late — *I've seen it.*

"I didn't want to come back and disrupt your life. You seemed happy... I didn't want to ruin that."

Her anger flares. "Leave my past out of this, Rodrigo."

"I'm not trying to dredge up the past. I didn't expect... any of this."

"A mistake, right? Is that what I am to you? Always have been."

"No, Petra. No. You were never a mistake. I'm sorry I ever made you feel that way. When I decided to come back to Seattle, it was just for business. I wasn't expecting... wasn't looking for this."

Her voice is a painful reminder. "Yeah, you don't do relationships, remember?"

"No, it's not that. I never thought I was enough for you," I confess.

"Playing the pity card now? Typical."

I gather my thoughts, "Seeing you again, it hit me hard. It was like a floodgate opened. I didn't plan for these feelings. But—"

She interrupts, her voice breaking. "I loved you, Rodrigo. And you just walked away. And now, you're back, playing the same games."

LOVED. The past tense echoes in my head.

"I'm not playing games, Petra. That's the truth," I insist, rising to stand before her.

"Sure, feels like a game to me."

I step closer, but she retreats. "Please, just talk to me."

"You lost that privilege," she fires back, turning to leave.

I step in front of her, blocking her escape. My voice is raw with desperation. "I know I don't deserve it. But I'm begging you, Petra. Just this once. Let's talk."

Tears stream down her face, a testament to the pain I've caused. I close the distance between us, pulling her into an embrace. She resists initially, but slowly, she yields, sinking into the comfort I offer, her body trembling with suppressed sobs.

Damn, I never meant for any of this.

"I'm really sorry, Bird," I whisper, my chin resting on her head. There's a quiet shift in her as she begins to settle down, still in my arms.

In a voice so faint it's almost lost, she admits, "I don't know what to feel."

"I know," I reply, my voice low. I try to pull back to look at her, but she's turning away, hiding her tears. "Hey, look at me," I ask gently.

Stubborn as ever, Petra shakes her head. So, I do what I can — I tilt her chin up, craving just a glimpse of those eyes. She's still dodging my gaze, so I plant a gentle kiss on her forehead, trying to bridge the distance between us with that small gesture. I take her hand, leading her to the couch, like we're navigating some kind of emotional minefield.

We slump onto the couch, the TV flickering in the background, casting shadows across us. She's miles away, lost in thought. "It's late... I should go," she mutters.

I can't let her leave, not like this. Gripping her hand, I plead, "Stay, please." It's a shot in the dark, but when she finally looks at me, eyes rimmed with runny eyeliner, there's a flicker of something. "Just stay here, with me," I push a little more, seeing her indecision. "We'll camp out on the couch for now, alright? Just...stay."

She tries to speak, but the words are like ghosts, barely there. A silent nod is all she gives, her gaze slipping away again.

In the stretch of silence that follows, it's like we're both lost in a sea of unsaid things. Then, she voices a practical concern, "But I've got work tomorrow... no clothes."

"I'll take care of it. I'll drop by Pedro's place in the morning, grab what you need before my flight."

Her response is quiet, just a nod, but her hand stays in mine. It's like a quiet 'yes' to my unspoken request. We're both adrift, but for now, at least, we're adrift together.

—

Petra's crashed on my couch, looking like a sleeping beauty with Saskya, the furry bodyguard, curled at her feet. I'm doing this slow, rhythmic hair-stroking thing, watching her breathe peacefully.

This night? Totally not what I expected. Thanks, wine.

But seeing her all serene and zonked out? There's something oddly comforting about it.

Her phone's throwing a mini rave on the coffee table, buzzing non-stop. Names like Yara, Deborah, Pedro flashing on the screen. Curiosity's biting, but I'm not playing peeping Tom tonight. Instead, I whip out my phone for some damage control, texting Pedro, "Petra's with me. She's fine. Crashed at my place. Don't freak out. Details later. Need to grab her stuff from your place in the morning. No Q&A session now."

Pedro's on it like white on rice. "What's up? Deb and I texted, but there was no reply. Radio silence. Getting worried."

"She's out like a light, hence the no-reply situation."

"Everything's cool, though, right?" Pedro's clearly not great at the whole 'no questions' thing.

"Just chill, Pedro. We'll talk tomorrow," I try to shut it down.

"Gotcha," he finally backs off. Phone goes back in my pocket. I lean back, eyes shut for a sec.

Next thing I know, it's 4 a.m. Petra's still out, head on my lap, Saskya still playing guard dog. I give Petra's shoulder a nudge, and she makes this adorable little groan. Saskya's all tail wags and excitement, but I shush her with a finger.

Time to relocate Sleeping Beauty. I scoop up Petra, trying not to wake her. She's probably beat from all the crying. Lights off with the elbow, up the stairs we go, Saskya in tow.

In my room, I flick the light on – elbow again, feeling like some sort of ninja – and lay Petra down. Heels off, blanket on. Saskya's giving me the big puppy eyes, jumping onto the bed. I shoot her the 'you know better' look, but she's pulling the guilt trip, resting her head on Petra's arm. "Alright, fine. This one time," I whisper.

Saskya settles next to Petra, who stirs but then finds her way back to dreamland. I make sure everything's cozy for her before I hit the lights and head out, closing the door softly behind me.

I tiptoe to the bathroom near my bedroom – no way am I cranking up the shower and risking waking Sleeping Beauty. Quick freshen up, nothing fancy. Then, it's joggers and a tee for me – gotta keep it comfy.

Back in my room, Petra and Saskya are all snuggled up on my bed. Feels weirdly right. I slide in, careful not to jostle them. Staying on top of the covers, I sneak my arm around Petra. It's a bold move, but it feels... natural?

Eyes shut, I let the fatigue take over. Drifting off, my mind's replaying the night's craziness – the wine, the tears, the unplanned intimacy. Petra here, in my bed, with all those unspoken things hanging in the air.

It's a mess, but for now, I'm just gonna ride the wave of whatever this is.

CHAPTER TWENTY-FIVE

PETRA

Waking up feels like a train's just plowed through my head. Sun's blasting through the window, and oh boy, am I feeling last night. Then it hits me – I'm in Rodrigo's bed, wrapped up like a burrito in this blanket. He's right here, arm around me, but he's not under the blanket.

I shift a bit, and there's this weight on my legs. Squinting, I spot Saskya, out cold. I need my phone, but it's playing hide and seek. Not in my pocket, not on the nightstand. Then the real panic sets in – work, messages, the usual life stuff I've seemingly abandoned since stepping into this alternate reality called 'spending the night at Rodrigo's.'

As I squirm, trying to locate my elusive phone, Rodrigo wakes up. His voice, groggy with sleep, cuts through the silence. "You okay, Bird?" he mumbles.

"Just on a phone hunt," I whisper back.

Saskya's awake now, tail thumping like a drum solo.

"Phone's downstairs. My bad, left it in the living room." He's still holding onto me.

"What time is it?" I ask, curious.

He grabs his phone, "6:45 am. Alarm's set for 7. I gotta swing by Pedro and Deborah's for your stuff."

"I can do that," I offer.

"Nah, I already told Pedro. Just give me the fashion brief," he says.

"Oh, so you're a fashion guru now?"

He chuckles, "Almost went into fashion design, believe it or not."

"Sure, Rodrigo, sure."

He goes on, "It's easy. Your wardrobe's like a monochrome mood board – black, white, beige, grey, brown. I'll just pick something black or beige."

"Okay, fashionista, maybe I should tag along."

He whispers, all smug, "Fancy a ride in my 'humble' car before 8?"

"Your 'humble' BMW?" I rib him. "Yeah, I'm coming. No way you're playing dress-up with my closet. I'll end up at work in a mini skirt and sneakers."

"You don't do mini skirts," he says, all confident.

I twist to look at him, "And how would you know?"

"I just do. Call it a talent."

"Alright, Mr. Fashion Expert, I'm coming with. Just to save myself from your 'excellent' fashion choices," I say, deciding I'm definitely riding shotgun on this outfit rescue mission.

Rodrigo's rocking these beige dress pants and a black polo, topped off with his sneakers. I catch myself checking out his footwear before our eyes meet. "What? Gotta stay comfy for the New York flight. It's a marathon, not a sprint," he defends.

"I didn't say a word," I shoot back.

"But you were thinking it," he says with that grin of his.

We shuffle downstairs. I pick my phone, swamped with notifications, and freshen up Saskya's setup. Then it's off to Pedro and Deborah's in Rodrigo's ride – gotta circle back here after the clothes heist.

We pull up at their place, and as soon as we hit their floor, I can tell it's all systems go inside. Pedro and Deborah are probably in full morning hustle mode.

"Hey!" Deborah's all energy, heels clicking, blonde waves dancing around her white blazer. She's straight in for the hug. "Girl, where were you?"

"I'm fine," I reassure her, "Just came for some clothes."

She steps back, giving me the once-over. "You with Rodrigo last night?"

Rodrigo pops in, "Present and accounted for." He waves.

"I see," she says, playfully jabbing him. Then, back to me, "Your makeup's all over the place. Tears?"

"No, no," I deflect, "Just slept in it."

"Why at his place?"

"Oh, you know, Rodrigo needed someone for Saskya while he's in New York," I fib, "We had dinner, I crashed. Long day and all."

Deborah's about to dive deeper, but Rodrigo cuts in, "Love this interrogation, really, but I've got a plane to catch. Ladies, can we wrap up the soap opera?"

Deborah lets it slide. "Fine, but we're not done here. You and me, dinner tonight."

"Deal," I agree.

Rodrigo chimes in, "Just don't forget about Saskya, okay? She needs her walks."

"I'll bring her to dinner. Now, let me grab my stuff."

Deborah nods, and then here comes Pedro, all brotherly concern. "Petty! You good?"

I'm enveloped in a bear hug.

"You'd think I kidnapped her or something." Rodrigo teases.

Deborah's quick to fire back, "Given your history, it's a bit weird, no?"

Rodrigo just looks at her and I jump in, "We'll catch up later, I promise. Right now, I gotta grab my things and head back before work."

"Okay," Deborah accepts it. "Dinner, remember."

"I won't forget. And Saskya's coming too."

After I gather my stuff – clothes, toothbrush, and trusty hair detangler – Rodrigo and I zip back to his place. He's got a flight to catch to New York, and we're on a tight schedule.

As soon as we hit the door, Saskya's all wiggles and excitement. Rodrigo drops to her level, giving her the full-on 'dad's leaving' spiel. "Behave for Petra, okay?" He's got this soft spot for her that's kind of adorable. "I'll miss you, girl. Stay out of trouble."

He stands, turning to me, "Thanks for doing this. Really means a lot."

"She's easy. No problem."

He's all serious for a sec. "Just, uh, keep her off the bed, alright?"

I raise an eyebrow, "But this morning...?"

He grins, "Exception. Special circumstances. We had a deal, didn't we, Saskya?"

I nod with a smile, "Alright, bed's a no-go zone."

He grabs his suitcase, all set to go, then pauses, giving me this look that's got more layers than an onion. "I'll miss you too, Bird." That catches me off guard.

Rodrigo? Mr. 'Keep-It-Cool'? I'm momentarily speechless.

As I find my voice, he's already halfway out the door. "Text me when you land," I manage.

He gives me this warm, genuine smile. "You got it."

Ava nods, totally getting it. "Jet lag's a beast."

I remember Petra's message. "Oh, Ava, Petra says hi."

Jax perks up, "Petra?"

I shoot him a look. "Not for your ears, Jax. Ava's the one in the Petra fan club."

Ava laughs. "Yeah, she's a gem. Always checking up on me."

Jax's curiosity's piqued now. "Who's Petra?"

Ava glances my way, "I didn't mention anything to you about her because I thought it was a topic Rodrigo would bring up."

"Ava, stop making it look like Petra and I are running off to Vegas to elope."

Jax's eyes widen. "Wait, are you two an item now?"

Ava spills the beans. "You remember the girl with no name. Seattle girl?"

Jax connects the dots. "The one you messed up with?"

I interject. "Love how I'm being discussed like I'm not here. Do go on, it's like watching a reality show about my life."

Ava confirms Jax's guess, nibbling her lip.

Jax's like a kid in a candy store. "So, you're back on?"

I take a deep breath. "No, Jax. Ava's just hyping it up. Petra's around because of work stuff. She works for my father and brother, and now also with me because of a business agreement we have due to our companies merging."

"What?"

"Yeah, bro. It's a long story. Buckle up for some serious catch-up time."

Hours later, after an info-marathon with Jax, my jet-lagged brain's waving the white flag. Food's the last thing on my mind.

"I think I'm gonna pass on dinner, guys. My body's still on Seattle time. How about I head to my place, settle in, and we regroup later?"

Ava's understanding as always. "Sure thing. I'll drive you back."

Hopping into the car with Ava, we cruise through the New York streets. "Thanks for the lift," I say as we pull up to my building. She gives me a 'no problem' kind of smile, and I head up to my apartment, perched high on the 15th floor. Stepping inside, it feels like a homecoming.

I've barely kicked off my shoes when my phone buzzes with Petra's updates. Two notifications. First up, a pic of Saskya looking all adorable with a caption that reads, "Your baby is safe. Came home early to work and hang with Sask before dinner with aunt Dee." That brings a grin to my face. Then there's a selfie – Petra and Saskya. Petra's killing it in white high-waisted trousers, a beige V-neck, and a cream blazer, looking like a fashion magazine come to life. "And because you asked, here are the two ladies. PS: You would never be able to put this outfit together." My smile lingers, and I'm glad no one's here to catch me grinning like an idiot at my phone.

I quickly type a response, "For your information, I could totally one-up that outfit." With a chuckle, I place my phone on the entrance table, leaving it behind as I wander deeper into the apartment.

Outside, New York's night sky is turning inky, but the city lights keep the darkness at bay. They're like thousands of fireflies, twinkling away. Seattle's my home, but man, this view from my New York place? It's something else – a piece of my heart I miss every time I'm away.

But then, thoughts of Seattle, of home, and Petra, with her sass and undeniable charm, pull me back. It's a tug-of-war between two worlds – one here in this electric city and the other, softer and quieter, in the arms of someone who's unexpectedly become a significant part of my life. *Again.*

Rodrigo Miller Gomez, caught in a sentimental dilemma.

Life's got a weird sense of humor.

—

PETRA

As I clip Saskya's leash on and shrug into my coat, I'm already mentally bracing for dinner with Deborah. The whole Rodrigo's-house-for-a-week thing? It's like living in someone else's skin, and it's weirdly intimate in a way that's hard to pin down. I mean, it's Rodrigo's house. His space. And here I am, about to play house with his dog.

And then there's the whole 'what-the-heck-are-we-doing' thing with Rodrigo. Last night was like a whirlwind – he's here, then he's off to New York, and we're left with this big, unspoken... something. It's like we're dancing around each other, and the music's stopped, but neither of us knows how to leave the dance floor.

Plus, my phone's blowing up. Yara's in full pregnancy panic mode, and let's not even start on Douglas. It's like my life decided to become a TV Show without asking me first.

I give Saskya a whistle and head out, thoughts swirling like a storm. It's chilly outside, the kind of cold that bites at your cheeks, so I'm glad for the extra layer. Saskya's all excited, tail wagging like she's about to embark on the greatest adventure of her life. If only she knew we're just going for a quick stroll before I dive headfirst into an evening of interrogation with Deborah.

I walk into Deborah's place, and the smell of dinner hits me like a welcome hug. "Hey there," she calls out, all smiles and domestic goddess vibes.

"Hey!" I greet back, trying to match her cheer. "Need any help?"

"Nah, all under control. Pedro's bailed for the night, something about a dad dinner."

"Alright, cool." I shrug off my coat, hanging it up.

Deborah's not one to beat around the bush. "Spill. What's up with you and Rodrigo?"

"What do you mean?"

Innocent, who, me?

"Don't play dumb. You crashed at his place, remember?" She's giving me that 'I'm onto you' look.

"Yeah, but it's not what you think," I deflect, feeling my defenses rise.

"I call bullshit. You cried last night, didn't you?" She's got that mother-hen concern in her eyes, making it hard to keep up my guard.

And there it is – the elephant in the room. Last night, Rodrigo, the tears... It's all laid out like a puzzle I don't quite know how to solve. How do you explain something when you're still trying to figure it out yourself?

"Dee, come on," I chuckle, trying to lighten the mood as I see her eyes widen with every revelation. "Yes, I cried. Rodrigo and I, well, we sort of had an argument. And yes, I stayed over, but that's it. Just a sleepover. Pinky swear." I add the last part with a mock-serious face, fingers crossed behind my back for good measure.

"Girl, you're holding out on me. Spill the beans. There's gotta be more than just a sleepover."

"Okay, fine. The truth is, Rodrigo and I... well, we used to be a thing. Before he went off to Spain, we were close. Really close. But then, kaboom! Big fight, lots of drama, and poof – he vanished from my life." I admit, feeling a bit exposed.

Deborah's eyes light up like Christmas. "I knew something was up!" She's practically bouncing in her seat when she stops, "Hold up, you and Rodrigo? Seriously? Why am I only hearing about this now?"

I let out a sigh, raking a hand through my hair. "Yeah, it's complicated. We were... something. We were actually in a relationship, but not exactly an official one. It was intense, fiery, all-consuming. But then everything just blew up. Misunderstandings, harsh words, you name it. And just like that, poof – he was out of my life – radio silence for years."

"So, that's the backstory? Suddenly, all the weird vibes between you two make a ton of sense." Deborah leans in.

"Yeah, I guess so. With work forcing us together, we had to find some common ground. Surprisingly, it's been... less awful than I thought it would be."

"And all this led to last night?" Deborah's eyes twinkle, digging for more.

"Well, he had this trip to New York, and I somehow ended up agreeing to dog-sit Saskya there. And since you're so anti-dog in your pristine apartment," I say, throwing her a playful glare, "I ended up at his place."

"Alright, I get that. But the tears, what's up with that?" She's not letting anything slide.

Rubbing the back of my neck, I confess, "We had dinner, drank a bit too much wine, and then... we kissed." I can feel my face burning up just saying it out loud.

Deborah nearly jumps out of her chair. "You two kissed?!"

"Dee, please! Not so loud!" I whisper-yell, mortified.

"Sorry, sorry," she says, trying to contain her excitement. "But you can't leave me hanging. What happened next?"

I take a deep breath, feeling a little vulnerable. "It was just one kiss. But it opened up a whole can of worms. We got into this big argument about everything that went down years ago. And, yeah, I might've had a bit of a breakdown."

"I knew there was more to this story!" Deborah's practically glowing. "You and Rodrigo, after everything that's happened..."

"Can we please focus on dinner now?" I try to change the subject.

"Fine, we'll eat. But you're not escaping this conversation. There's more to unpack here, and I'm not letting you off the hook that easy."

"Fine, but let's at least eat." I say, swiftly steering the conversation away from my tangled feelings.

CHAPTER TWENTY-SIX

RODRIGO

A week in New York flew by as quickly as a shooting star. Petra's been my daily fix of cute, bombarding me with Saskya pics and those stealthy selfies she sneaks in. Always with Saskya, though. *Petra flying solo in a photo? As if.*

Ava and Jax have been my dynamic duo, like Sherlock and Watson, but cooler. Ava's sticking it out in New York, playing the boss lady. She's like a whirlwind in heels, handling Jax and work like it's child's play. I tried to get her to hit pause, but nope. That girl's work ethic is a force of nature.

Now, I'm on the brink of heading back to Seattle. It's a cocktail of excitement and dread, honestly. Eager to see Petra and untangle whatever's brewing between us, especially after that last night. But the thought of round two with jetlag? Not so thrilling. Taking off at 1 p.m., touching down at 3 p.m. – it's a time-traveling headache. Five hours in the sky, and I'll be more zombie than human.

I tap out a text to Petra, "Flight's in 2. Brace yourself for a hug that's Oscar-worthy. Maybe throw in a parade and the city keys for good measure?"

Her response zips back, "No can do. Boss would have my head if I played hooky for your grand entrance."

"Maybe I need to have a word with this boss of yours."

"He's a rule freak. Plus, your charm might be too much for him to handle."

"Come on, it's Friday. Surely he'll let you off the hook early. Also, aren't you breaking some rule by texting on the job?"

Back she fires, "First off, it's past 8. Blame the pup for my late start. Secondly, the boss is in the room as we speak. Say 'hi', boss."

I chuckle. "Got it, back to work you go. I'm off to brave the friendly skies."

"Fly safe," she replies.

"Will let the pilot know, Bird," I quip, ending our chat with a smile.

Seattle, here I come.

—

PETRA

I chuckle as I set my phone down, but before I can deep dive into my emails, my phone rings. It's Bea.

"What's up? You missing me?" I ask, my tone light, expecting the usual banter.

"Uh, not exactly," Bea's voice comes through, "Some guy came looking for you. Avery told him you weren't here, then... well, she gave him directions to Rodrigo's office."

I frown, perplexed. "A guy? My clients usually have the common sense not to turn up unannounced. They're supposed to go through Pedro, Rodrigo, or Mr. Gomez. What is this, a stalker casting call?"

"Yeah, he definitely didn't give off client vibes, Petty. But since he asked for you, Avery thought–" she trails off.

"Wait a minute. So, Avery's handing out my location like it's the last piece of candy on Halloween? Did she even bother to get this guy's name? Or was she too thrilled by the mystery?"

Bea hesitates, "He didn't say his name."

"So, just to be clear," I clarify, "A nameless, potentially creepy guy shows up, and Avery hands him a map to me. Fabulous."

"I knew you'd be upset. That's why I called."

Despite myself, I'm intrigued. "So, what did Mr. Mystery look like?"

She chuckles, "Well, at least he's easy on the eyes. If you're going to be stalked, at least it's by a handsome guy."

I snort. Fantastic. If I'm going to be abducted, at least it's by someone who could grace the cover of a magazine. Didn't Bea read enough thrillers or binge-watch enough crime shows? This is like a trope straight out of those.

She details his appearance, "Tall, hazel eyes, light brown hair..."

My mind races. *Doug?*

"Petra? You still with me?" Bea's voice pulls me from my thoughts.

"Yeah, just... trying to figure out this whole thing." I reply, "I guess I'll be playing host to an unexpected visitor. Don't worry, I'll take a selfie with my potential kidnapper for the memories."

Bea's concern is in the room. "Just... be safe, okay? And keep me in the loop."

—

The hours tick away like a slow dance, and by the time 5 p.m. rolls around, it's pretty clear my mysterious 'stalker' has either chickened out or, plot twist, it wasn't Doug after all. Looks like I've dodged a bullet.

Needing a break from my desk, I decide to treat myself to a mini getaway – coffee break style. I score a steaming ristretto from the Nespresso machine – my caffeine knight in shining armor.

I'm savoring my coffee, soaking in the Seattle sunset, when suddenly, a voice cuts through the moment. "Hi, Pet," it says, and it's like a record scratch in my head.

I whip around and, holy plot twist, it's really Douglas, grinning like he's won the big prize. My brain short-circuits – here I am, ristretto in hand, gaping like a fish.

"I wasn't sure if I should come here," he says, breaking the awkward silence.

"You really shouldn't have," I shoot back sharply.

He takes a cautious step closer, a frown creasing his forehead. "You've been ghosting my messages. And Yara's."

I raise an eyebrow, my tone dripping with sarcasm. "Ever wonder why? Maybe because I didn't want to hear from you?"

"Pet, we need to talk. You know we do," he insists.

I step back, putting space between us, my voice firm. "No, Douglas. We don't need to talk. We've said everything that needed to be said."

"But I need to explain," he pleads, his voice rising slightly in desperation.

"I don't give a flying fuck about your explanations," I snap, turning to leave.

"I screwed up, okay? I made a mistake," he persists.

I spin on my heel, fire in my eyes. "A mistake? Ditching us for some bimbo with a boob job? Seriously, Doug? That's what you call a mistake?"

He looks down, then back at me, "What do you want me to say, Pet? I know I screwed up. I was an idiot. But I'm here to make it right."

"I want you to leave. That's what I want." I reply bluntly. "I didn't ask for this reunion tour. You shouldn't even be here."

"Pet, please. Just hear me out."

I feel my anger boiling over. "I don't need to hear anything from you! You've said enough! And your move, using Yara's pregnancy to get close to me? That's pathetic. Even for you, Doug." I turn to walk away, my heart pounding. But he grabs my arm, and I shove him away with all my strength. "Don't you dare touch me," I hiss.

In that heated moment, Rodrigo appears, his presence like a sudden storm. He pushes Douglas away, standing firmly between us. "I believe the lady said 'no'," he growls, eyes locked on Douglas.

"And who the fuck are you?" Douglas sneers, clearly miffed at Rodrigo's interruption.

Rodrigo's unruffled as ever, "The owner of this building, so I suggest you leave before I call security."

Douglas chuckles, all smug. "Oh, I get it. Petra's moved on to a richer model, huh?" He smirks at me, as if Rodrigo's invisible.

"Get the hell out of here, Doug," I recommend.

Douglas can't resist a parting shot, so he throws a venomous parting shot, loud and clear. "Once a whore, always a whore."

Before I can even snap back, Rodrigo's on him like a hawk on prey. "You're gonna eat those words," he snarls, his voice a dangerous rumble.

"Rodrigo, don't!" I try to pull him back. "He's not worth it."

But Rodrigo's beyond hearing. His fists are clenched, eyes blazing, ready to unleash hell. Douglas, smirking like the devil himself, isn't backing down. He takes a swing at Rodrigo, who dodges with a growl.

"Please, stop!" I'm shouting now, pulling at Rodrigo's arm, trying to drag him back. "This isn't worth it!"

It's like trying to hold back a tidal wave. Rodrigo's entire body is tensed, ready to explode. Douglas, equally fired up, throws another punch, narrowly missing Rodrigo. I'm right there, in the thick of it, my heart pounding, trying to shove them apart.

"Enough!" I scream, my voice cracking. I finally get a hold of Rodrigo's jacket, yanking him back with all my might. Douglas, seizing the moment, tries to land another cheap shot.

Rodrigo ducks and swings, his fist connecting with Douglas's jaw with a sickening thud. Douglas stumbles, but he's not down for the count. He lunges again, aiming for Rodrigo, who's now fully engaged in this street brawl.

I'm screaming, pleading, "Stop it! Both of you!" But it's like they're in another world.

Just when I think it can't get any worse, Rodrigo grabs Douglas by the collar, slamming him against the nearest wall. Douglas, wild-eyed, fights back, but Rodrigo's got the upper hand.

I'm practically hanging off Rodrigo's arm, my voice almost drowned out in the chaos. "Rodrigo, for the love of

God! Let's just go!" I'm shouting, wedging myself between these two testosterone-charged bulls.

Rodrigo's eyes are like a storm, but they soften when he sees me, right in the thick of it. He freezes, "Petra, don't ever jump into the line of fucking fire like that!"

I'm trying to calm down, tears of frustration welling up. "I told you to stop."

He takes a deep, shuddering breath, his gaze snapping back to Douglas. "Leave, now. Or I'll regret what comes next."

Douglas smirks, trying to rile him up. "Tough words, big guy."

I grab Rodrigo's arm, giving him the 'don't-you-dare' look. "Ignore him, Rod. He's just baiting you."

The crowd's growing, eyes glued to our personal novella. Rodrigo scans the faces, then his eyes lock on mine.

"Let's go inside," I say, feeling like a mouse next to his lion.

"No, we're leaving. Now," he says, taking my hand and leading me through the sea of onlookers. "Show's over, folks," he barks at them, then to me, "Pack your things, Bird. We're done here."

I try to protest. "Rodrigo, I'm still clocked in—"

"I don't give a damn. Get your laptop. We're out."

"Where to?" I ask, shutting down my computer.

"Home," he says, a hint of steel in his voice.

I sigh, grabbing my stuff. "Fine."

I follow him out, a tornado of emotions swirling inside me as we leave the office behind.

—

The tension's thick as we drive, the silence only broken by Petra's sudden question. "Does it hurt?" she asks, her eyes flicking over to me.

I'm puzzled for a moment. "What hurts?"

"Your hand," she says, nodding towards the steering wheel. I glance down and notice my knuckles, raw and bloody.

"Oh, that," I say, brushing it off, "I'm fine."

"You shouldn't have done that."

I snap back locking my eyes on her for a second, "And why the fuck not?"

"Just keep your eyes on the road, Rodrigo," she commands, gently turning my head forward. "And... because he's not worth it."

"Yeah, but he touched you. He insulted you. You think I'd just stand by and let that happen?" My voice is bitter.

"Stop being mad at me," she fires back, irritation clear in her voice.

I take a deep breath and reply, "You sure know how to pick them."

"Oh, so now my taste in men is under fire? That's saying a lot."

I let out a sigh, not bothering to reply.

"I could have handled it myself," she adds, her voice rising.

"Sure thing." I mutter dismissively. "What were you doing with him anyway?"

"He just showed up," she shrugs.

"Just like that? He just popped up?"

"He's been texting me," she admits coldly.

I pull the car over in frustration. "You've been talking to him?" I turn to face her.

"I didn't say I replied," she snaps, crossing her arms.

"That's why he was there."

"Why didn't you tell him to get lost then?" I ask, trying to meet her gaze.

"I didn't want to deal with him," she mumbles, looking away.

"Great solution," I scoff.

"What do you want from me, Rodrigo? Mad if I talk, mad if I don't?"

I take another deep breath. "How did he even know where you were?"

"He's my ex," she reminds me, annoyance seeping through.

"I didn't need a reminder."

"Then stop asking stupid questions," she fires back. "He is my ex. I've worked with Pedro and your father for years now. I was with Douglas at the time. Maybe that's how he knows where I work or used to work, don't you think?"

"Jesus, this hostility." I tease before starting to drive again.

—

Once home, Saskya acts like I've returned from a decade-long expedition. After a mandatory petting session, I check my phone. It's buzzing like a beehive — texts from Ava and Jax, and, oh look, a missed call marathon from my brother.

Petra's already disappeared upstairs, so I give Pedro a ring back. He picks up, and man, is he on fire. "Rodrigo, what the hell? A street brawl, really? Have you lost it?"

I lean against the wall, playing it cool. "News travels fast."

"People talk, man. Even Dad's caught wind of it," he warns.

"Can't say I care much," I respond, casually tossing my keys on the table.

"Is that right?" He sounds skeptical.

"Let me guess, they only gave you the Hollywood version? Just the action, no context?"

"Just the fight, yeah. Heard you almost rearranged some guy's face while Petra was there too."

"Yeah, her charming ex, Douglas, decided to grace us with his presence. I was just back from the flight."

"Douglas? As in...?" He trails off.

"Yeah, Pedro, as in Donald Duck. Who else? Unless she's got a line of exes I'm not aware of."

"What did he want?" Pedro's tone turns serious.

"He was getting handsy with Petra. She told him off, he didn't listen, so I helped him understand," I recall, my hands balling into fists.

"Man, you can't pull stunts like that. You're the boss..."

"Pedro, I don't give a damn about appearances. Tell me you wouldn't do the same for Deborah?" I challenge him.

"Sure, I would, but Deborah's my fiancée. What's your excuse?"

Damn him.

Touché, brother. Touché.

CHAPTER TWENTY-SEVEN

PETRA

Rodrigo strides into the bedroom, Saskya padding along behind him like his shadow. I'm in the middle of cramming my clothes into my bag, intent on bolting back to Pedro and Deborah's apartment. "What's the hurry, Bird?" Rodrigo asks, his voice casual as he watches me stuff my shirts with a bit more force than necessary.

"Just... getting ready to head back," I reply, avoiding his gaze and focusing on a particularly stubborn zipper.

He moves closer, his hand finding my arm in a gentle but firm grip. His touch is warm, almost too warm, as if it could melt all the ice I've been piling up inside. "Why so fast?" he asks, his fingers lightly caressing my arm.

I look down at his hand, then up at him. "I was supposed to stay until you got back, and well, you're back," I say, trying to sound matter-of-fact. I try to shift my attention back to my bag, but his gaze is like a magnet.

"There's no rule saying you can't stay longer."

"Rodrigo, that's not a good idea."

His eyebrow arches, "What's up? You look tense."

"I'm fine," I lie, my voice a little sharper than I intend.

He smirks, "I know 'fine' Petra and 'I'm-so-not-fine' Petra. This is definitely the latter."

"Rodrigo, really, I'm fine." The zipper of my bag gives a satisfying snap as it closes.

He leans in, his voice insistent but soft, "Talk to me. What's got you all in a knot?"

I sigh, "What do you want me to say, Rodrigo?"

"Well, one thing I know for sure – I didn't expect to come home to you mad at me."

I stop packing, my hands hovering over the bag, "And I didn't expect to see you turn into a street fighter outside the office."

He frowns, "Are you mad about me decking Douglas?"

"It's not about the punches, Rodrigo."

"Then what is it? He insulted you–"

"Yes, he did. But I could have handled it. I don't need a knight in shining armor."

He raises his voice, "So, you're upset because I stepped in?"

"I didn't need you to," I say, avoiding his gaze. "You shouldn't have."

His voice softens, "Petra, I–"

"No, Rodrigo. Just... no," I interrupt, picking up my bag and heading towards the door.

"I just couldn't stand by and watch him talk to you like that, Petra."

"Yeah, right," I mutter.

He looks at me, his agitation growing. "What's eating at you? This doesn't make sense."

I spin around, facing him, "You know what's really nonsensical? This–" I gesture between us, "–us. We've been texting non-stop, like there's something more, and now here we are, arguing over you playing the hero with my ex. It's all just... it doesn't add up."

"You're right. We need to sort this out. But every time I try, you run."

"How convenient for you."

He leans in, "You wanna know why I really punched him?"

"Because he insulted me. We've been over this."

Rodrigo nods, his tone shifting to something more serious. "Pedro called me out as soon as we got here. Apparently, word travels fast about a CEO brawling in the streets. He was freaking out about the company's image, about what people would say. And the funny thing? I didn't give a shit."

I stay silent, listening for once.

"I've always cared about my image, about the company's reputation. But in that moment, none of it mattered. The only thing that did was you, Petra. Standing up for you, protecting you. And I'd do it again, status be damned," he confesses.

I'm speechless, caught off guard by his raw honesty.

He continues, "Being with you, Petra, it's made me rethink my priorities. My company is everything to me, but you... you're something else. You've turned my world upside down."

I barely whisper, "I don't know what to say."

"Pedro's reaction made me realize how much you mean to me. I asked him if he wouldn't do the same for Deborah. And that's when it hit me. I can't keep making excuses for how I feel about you."

"But Deborah is his fiancée."

He nods and laughs, "Yeah, that's what he said. But for me, excuses are over." He takes my hands in his, looking at me with an intensity that sends my heart racing. "I can't pretend anymore. I care about you, Petra, more than I've let on. When I found out about your relationship, it hit me hard. Ava and Jax, they've known about you for a long time, even before you walked into my office that day."

"Rodrigo," I start, but he stops me.

"Let me finish, please, love." He's close now, "I know I've got a bit of a... image, but honestly, these last six years, there's been no one else for me. Not really. You've been there, in my head, haunting every quiet moment. Whether I was in Spain, New York, wherever – you were the one I couldn't shake off."

I'm stunned, my mind reeling.

He takes a deep breath, "I should've said this a long time ago..." My heart feels like it's pounding out of my chest, "I've been carrying this around for over six years. Every day, I've regretted not telling you how much you mean to me, not showing you just how special you are."

I'm trembling. "Rodrigo, I..." I start, but my voice fails.

He steps closer, "Petra, I love you. Always have. I'm crap at showing it, but it's the truth. And I'm sorry for any moment I made you feel otherwise." He pulls me into a tight hug, his arms strong and reassuring around me. "I'm so sorry. And I want to make it right, make up for all those lost years." He pulls back slightly, a wry smile on his lips. "I know I've got no right to ask anything of you, but let's face it, I'm a selfish guy. I can't lose you again, Petra." I try to speak, to process all of this, but words fail me.

My mind's a whirlwind.

"You love me?" I blurt out, my voice an octave higher than normal, incredulity lacing every word. "After years of radio silence, this is your grand reveal?"

Rodrigo's laugh is a deep rumble, echoing around the room, filled with a warmth that belies the absurdity of the situation. "Yeah, I'm pretty bad with timing. But what can I say, Petra? It's the truth. Every word."

"You waltz back into my life, turn it upside down, and now drop a love bomb like it's nothing?"

His gaze softens, and there's a gentleness there that catches me off guard, "It's everything but nothing, Bird. You've always been my everything."

I raise an eyebrow, unable to suppress a smirk. "Still with the 'Bird'?"

"What? You prefer 'darling' or 'sweetheart'?" he teases, his lips curving up.

"I prefer 'real'," I shoot back, crossing my arms. "Cut the nicknames. Be real with me, Rod."

His eyes darken, the playful light in them shifting to something more intense, more serious. "Real, huh?" He steps closer, the heat from his body mingling with mine. "You want real? This is as real as it gets." His breath is warm against my cheek, his presence overwhelming. "I've been waiting to do this for too damn long."

Before I can react, his lips crash against mine, a perfect storm of pent-up desire and long-suppressed feelings. His hands find their place on my waist, pulling me impossibly close. My fingers tangle in his hair, anchoring myself to him in the whirlwind he's created.

We're lost in a world of our own, where the past collides with the present. It's a kiss that's been years in the making – rough, raw, and real.

As we finally break apart, gasping for air, Rodrigo rests his forehead against mine. "Was that real enough for you?" he murmurs, a half-smile playing on his lips.

"That was... definitely something."

His cocky smile widens. "Good. Because, Petra, I'm just getting started. I'm not done being real. Not by a long shot." He leans in again, his lips brushing mine in a teasing whisper. "I'm not good with words, Bird. But actions... that's where I excel."

"Show me then," I challenge, the words hardly a breath.

Rodrigo doesn't need to be told twice. His hands slide up my back, pulling me closer as his mouth claims mine with hunger. The kiss deepens, and I'm swept away by the intensity of it, by the way he makes me feel.

Our bodies press together, the heat between us building to an almost unbearable level. He breaks the kiss, trailing hot, urgent kisses down my neck, his breath ragged against my skin.

"Petra," he whispers, his voice thick. "You have no idea how long I've wanted this, how many times I've dreamed of having you like this."

My response is a moan, lost in the sensation of his touch. "Rodrigo—"

He cuts me off with another searing kiss, his hands roaming over me with a possessiveness that's as thrilling as it is terrifying. "No more talking," he says between kisses. "Just feel."

And I do. I feel every touch, every caress, as he peels away the layers between us.

His hands slide under my top, bold and sure, tracing the lines of my waist, making me hold my breath. It's like he's got a map of my body in his mind, and he's following it inch by inch.

He's smooth, *too smooth*, as he flicks open my bra with a magician's ease. In a heartbeat, he's got me on the bed, a blend of trouble and hunger in his eyes. It's like he's playing a game, and he doesn't want to lose.

Here I am, letting my top and bra just fall away. I'm laid bare, not just in skin, but everything. And when he peels off his shirt, whoa. The guy's ripped – not gym-ripped, but like he's been chiseled out of marble or something. *Greek God?* Definitely giving off those vibes.

Our eyes lock, and there's this sizzle. He's got his hands everywhere, and I mean everywhere, as we sprawl on his bed. It's like he's on a mission to know every inch of me, and honestly, I'm here for it. His fingers dance over my skin, light and teasing, but it's when he lowers his head to my chest that things really heat up.

His lips, *damn*, they're doing things to my nipples that should probably be illegal. It's a combination of soft and warm, gentle and totally mind-blowing. He's alternating between them, and every flick of his tongue, every little nibble, sends these shockwaves straight through me. I'm trying to keep it together, but it's Rodrigo – he knows exactly what he's doing.

And while he's busy driving me crazy up top, his other hand's on a different mission. He's undoing my pants, but it's like he's savoring every moment, every button, like he's unwrapping a present he's been dying to open. And when his hand finally slips inside, *oh boy*, it's like a bolt of lightning. It's hot, it's heavy, and it's got me thinking all kinds of things I probably shouldn't say out loud. But with this guy? It's always been like that – *just a touch, and I'm gone*.

As Rodrigo's fingers venture lower, teasing the heated skin between my thighs, I gasp. It's like something is sparking to life under his touch, brief but enough to send a wave of heat crashing through me. And here he goes, smirking like he's won a prize, knowing exactly how much he's affecting me.

He comes back up to kiss me, and it's like he's not just kissing me, but telling a story. His tongue dances with mine in a way that's just as teasing, just as daring as his wandering hands. It's a wild, and it's driving me absolutely crazy.

Then, he's sliding my pants off, real slow, like he's savoring every second, leaving me in just my panties, feeling every ounce of the electric air between us.

My hand finds its way to his abs, tracing down to the waistband of his pants. *And hello, Mr. Obvious* – he's just as into this as I am. That realization, feeling just how much he wants me, it's like a hit of the strongest aphrodisiac.

We lock eyes, and it's like a silent conversation, an understanding that words just can't touch. His eyes are dark, deep pools of want, and I'm drowning in them, lost in the need to be closer, to feel more.

As Rodrigo finally shimmies my pants off, it's like our bodies are doing all the talking. He gives me this look, you know, like he's admiring his favorite piece of art. Then he starts kissing down my belly, each kiss hotter and more promising than the last. He reaches my panties and, with that cheeky grin of his, just pulls them aside – no messing around.

He's all in, doing this thing with his tongue that's straight-up mind-blowing. It's like every flick, every touch, is flipping switches I didn't even know I had. I'm totally swept up in it, every nerve ending buzzing.

But just as I feel myself getting lost in the intensity, I give him a gentle nudge and crawl over to him. He stands up at the edge of the bed, looking like a snack. I take my time with his pants, making a show of it, and they hit the floor with a thud. *And man, he does not disappoint – he's all kinds of wow.*

I reach for him, feeling his arousal beneath my fingertips. I lean in, my mouth meeting him. It's hot, hungry, a total give-and-take.

The room fills up with the sounds of us, those heavy breaths and little moans. It's intense, real intense – like we're not just connecting bodies here, but something way deeper.

—

RODRIGO
TWO MONTHS LATER

"Whoa, hold up. Let me take care of this," I say, grabbing Petra's box of stuff like I'm on some mission. "Holy cow, what's in here, Bird? I almost forgot how much stuff you have."

Saskya's buzzing around us like some overexcited bee, trying to help but mostly just darting everywhere. She's like a ball of energy, bouncing between Petra and the car. I crack up when I hear Petra's laugh. Turning around, I see Saskya has tackled her to the ground. They're rolling in the grass, laughing like they don't have a care in the world.

I grin, scooping Saskya off Petra. "Let's give our girl some air? We can't have her getting smothered in all this adorableness."

"Jeez, Petra," Pedro chimes in, lugging another box. "Did you raid a mall or something? How much stuff does one person need?" Petra just chuckles and gives him a playful shove.

"I still don't get why you'd pick living with this guy over us," Deborah teases, acting like I'm not even here.

"Hey, I'm right here, you know," I shoot back with a grin.

"Sure, sure," Deborah says looking at me and then back at Petra. "But really, why? Is it the super-fancy coffee machine? The toilet seat warmer? His endless dad jokes?"

"It's definitely the coffee machine and the dog," Petra says, trying to keep a straight face. "Definitely not for his personality. Have you seen him in the morning? Trust me, he's a bigger grump than me pre-coffee. And that's saying something." They keep acting like I'm invisible.

We're all pitching in to help Petra get settled in, but let's be real – it's mostly Deborah and Petra doing the heavy lifting. Pedro and I are basically glorified doorstops, throwing in our two cents now and then. Honestly, I have no idea where anything goes, and I'm not sweating it. As long as Petra's happy, she can put her stuff wherever.

Finally, Petra steps back, hands on her hips, "Okay, that's it for now. The rest can wait."

Deborah pipes up, "Hungry much? How about we order some food?"

Dinner's a combination of random chit-chat and comfortable silences. Thinking back, it's crazy how things shifted – Petra moved in with Pedro and Deborah right when I got back from New York. We went from barely tolerating each other's presence to, well, her moving in with me.

It's been a wild ride, but I wouldn't change a thing.

Ava's back from New York too, with Jax in tow. They just got here this week. We're planning a dinner thing so Jax can meet Petra – the girl who actually got Rodrigo Gomez to commit. *Go figure.*

I catch myself staring at Petra, and when our eyes meet, she gives me this smile that just does things to me. She snuggles in closer, resting her head on my shoulder. It's like everything's clicking into place.

Deborah breaks the moment, "Okay, you two lovebirds. Time for us to scram and leave you alone."

Pedro adds with a naughty look, "Oh, and Mom's itching to have dinner with us soon. She's been nagging about seeing Petra again, and of course, giving Rodrigo a hard time for keeping her all to himself."

"Can't wait for more of Mom's teasing." I joke.

Petra chuckles and plants a soft kiss on my cheek, "Don't worry, I've got your back."

As Pedro and Deborah head out, I feel the luckiest guy in the world. Everything's just right, especially with Petra here.

She's more than just a part of my life – *she's become my home.*

EPILOGUE

PETRA
ONE YEAR LATER

"Hang tight, we're nearly there," I say, trying to keep Deborah from having a full-blown bridal meltdown as I zip up her wedding dress.

"Please tell me I haven't outgrown this dress. I'll legit freak out," Deborah panics.

"Dee, relax. The dress is perfection, and so are you in it," I assure her, just as Rodrigo barges in.

Deborah squeals, "No, Rodrigo! Bad luck to see the bride!"

I laugh and Rodrigo quips, "Look, as much as I'd love to be the groom, Deb, you're kinda stuck with my brother."

"I'm freaking out here," Deborah confesses, her hands doing this nervous dance.

"Dee, you've micromanaged every detail to death. What could possibly go wrong? You've got this." I give her a reassuring grin, "Plus, I'm rocking this beige silk number you picked out. Be happy about it!"

Rodrigo pipes up, "And let's talk about how smoking you look in that dress, Bird." He does this once-over that's all tease and trouble. "Good choice, Deb," he adds with a wink, earning a blush from both of us.

Deborah beams, "Thanks!"

Rodrigo, with his gaze on Deborah, says, "You're gonna knock Pedro off his feet. Seriously, you're a knockout."

Right on cue, Evelyn bursts in, mock-scolding him, "Rodrigo, scoot! You're supposed to be with Pedro, not crashing the bridal suite!" She chases him out with a laugh.

But Rodrigo, ever the rogue, swoops back in, steals a quick kiss on my cheek that sends my heart racing, and then he's out, leaving us all giggling.

Evelyn turns her attention to us, "Deborah, you're stunning," she says, enveloping her in a hug. Then she looks at me, eyes twinkling, "And Petra, in that dress? Breathtaking. Rodrigo's lucky to have you."

I'm totally blushing.

She gives me this knowing wink, "I wouldn't be surprised if Rodrigo puts a ring on your finger sooner than you think." And just like that she leaves me here, all flustered and daydreaming about, well, you know. She then announces, "Deborah's all set to become Mrs. Right!" We all cheer, hearts pounding as we head to the ceremony.

"You got this, girl," I whisper to Deborah, giving her hand a squeeze.

—

The reception is off the charts. Deborah and Pedro are just oozing love. Sofia, in her element, is snapping pics left and right, dragging me into a few. Even caught a candid of me and Rodrigo.

Speaking of Rodrigo – he's patching things up with his dad. Mr. Gomez is all smiles and pride, even had a heart-to-heart with me. Dropped the formalities and called me by my first name.

I KNOW, RIGHT? Felt like being welcomed into the fam. Evelyn, man, she's the mom everyone wishes they had. She's all over, showering everyone with love, me and Deborah included. Her vibe is just pure warmth.

Deborah's folks made the trek from California. They're beaming, watching their girl say 'I do'. I mean, who wouldn't be? It's a big deal.

As the night heats up, it's bouquet toss time. All the single ladies, myself included, gather. Can't skip this tradition. Rodrigo sneaks up beside me, whispering, "Catch it, don't catch it, doesn't matter to me." I shoot him a playful look and he grins, "But hey, go for it. Can't let Deborah's designer skills go to waste."

"Me catching this means we're next?" I wink at him.

He's about to answer when Deborah's voice cuts in, "Here goes nothing, ladies!"

I reach for the bouquet, but it slips through like it's got a mind of its own. Then I turn and see Rodrigo, bouquet in hand, looking like he's won the raffle. "Thought this might look better with you," he says, handing it over. He plants a sweet kiss on my forehead. "Bouquet or not, we both know where this is heading," he murmurs with that trademark smirk I love and hate at the same time.

ACKNOWLEDGMENTS

So, here we are, at the acknowledgments page of the second edition of "Trade Secret of a Messy Relationship." Can you believe it? Because I certainly can't! Republishing this book is like reliving a dream, and I'm over the moon about it.

First off, a huge, heart-swelling thanks to my mom. You know, she's the real MVP. She was always the first to dive into everything - the cover, the character art, the drafts - you name it. Her unwavering support and belief in my wild ideas have been my rock. MOM, YOU'RE THE STAR IN MY SKY.

Then there's my boyfriend, MY ROCK, MY SIDEKICK. This guy deserves a medal for sitting beside me (literally!) through the countless hours of writing and re-writing. His opinions and insights were like little nuggets of gold. Thanks for being my sounding board and for putting up with my writer's madness.

Okay, time for a bit of self-love. I need to give a shout-out to myself. Yeah, you heard that right! After long days at my job, I still found the energy to write, to chase this dream of being a full-time author. It wasn't easy, but hey, look where we are now!

And last, but oh so not least, my BOOKSTAGRAM FAM! You all are amazing. Every single one of you – the readers, the reviewers, the friends – you're the heart of this beautiful community. Your support means the world to me. This journey we're on? It's just getting started, and I can't wait to see where it takes us.

HERE'S TO MESSY RELATIONSHIPS, TRADE SECRETS, AND THE MAGIC OF STORYTELLING.

With all my love and gratitude,

FRANCES BLACKTHORN

ABOUT THE AUTHOR

Home is where the heart is, and for me, that's somewhere in the beautiful, diverse tapestry of EUROPE. I share this adventure with my boyfriend and our two furry little devils, who are as mischievous as they are adorable. It's a life filled with love, chaos, and endless inspiration.

Since I was a teenager, books have been my escape, my passion, and my best friends. I guess it was inevitable that I'd turn this lifelong love affair into a career. And here I am – a writer, living the dream one word at a time.

Coffee is my fuel. Seriously, I can't function without it. It's my magic potion that helps me conjure up all those words and stories.

When I'm not glued to my computer, weaving new tales, you can find me curled up watching horror movies. Yep, I love a good scare! But, I also have a soft spot for the dark, whimsical worlds created by the genius Tim Burton. His films are my guilty pleasures – they're like eerie fairy tales for grown-ups.

So, that's a little snapshot of me. A bookworm-turned-author, living a life filled with stories, coffee, a touch of sarcasm, and a whole lot of love.

THANKS FOR JOINING ME ON THIS JOURNEY.